WEDNESDAY RIDERS

By

TUDOR ROBINS

Island Trilogy – Book Two

Editor: Hilary Smith
Front cover design: Allie Gerlach
Proofreader: Gillian Campbell
Spine / back cover / interior design: Cheryl Perez
www.yourepublished.com
Website: Lynn Jatania / Sweet Smart Design www.sweetsmartdesign.com

ISBN: 978-0-9936837-3-2
Copyright 2015 Tudor Robins

Visit Tudor at www.tudorrobins.ca/

Also by Tudor Robins

Objects in Mirror

Appaloosa Summer

Dedication

This book is dedicated to all the horses I've loved, and who have inspired me. I can name a few of them – Willow, Chico, Killick, Lass, Rebel, William, Sun, Hazard, Duchess, Major, Jessie, Crombie, Martin – but there are many, many more out there. Each has been special in his or her own way.

Chapter One

The dress looked great at the store. Amazing in the full-length mirrors. Perfect in the filtered light of the changing room, with Slate standing behind me saying, "That's the one, Meg-girl!"

Now, at home, preparing to wear it to the prom tonight, I'm not so sure. "I think it's too short," I say.

"It's not too short, Meg. It's perfect."

"But …" I tap the skin left bare at mid-thigh.

"Uh-huh. You're showing your legs. Which are great." Slate turns me to the mirror, points at the high halter neckline. "And you're completely covered up here. No décolletage, no cleavage, no nothing."

"What does that even mean? Décolletage? It's such a grandma word."

Slate sighs. "It just means a low-cut neckline. And stop changing the subject. You're sexy on the bottom, classy on top; perfect for prom."

"But the fabric. It's so … slippery."

"It's not a cotton t-shirt, or stretch breeches. It's not running lycra. It's different. Which is good. You should look different tonight. This is *it*."

And she's right. It is. My symbolic end to high school. My launch into the rest of my life. Most importantly, my last night in the city. Tomorrow Jared and I drive to the island. Tomorrow I move back to the cottage and pick up my summer life again.

I've missed living at the cottage; having my horse just up the road instead of a half-hour's drive away. And, of course, having Jared just up the road, too. I've even missed my summer job at the Bed & Breakfast, working side-by-side with Betsy and Carl; more friends than bosses.

"OK, fine. I'll shut up. And I guess I'll wear it; it's not like I have another prom dress tucked away somewhere."

Slate claps her hands. "Oh yay! You know what this means; time to do your make-up. She hands me a scarf. "Put this around your shoulders to protect the dress just in case."

"How much make-up are you planning on using?"

"As much as I need."

I roll my eyes as she points to my desk chair, but I'm glad Slate's here. Happy we haven't drifted apart while she's been at university. I don't even mind that we don't ride together any more. Having different interests is good – it means she knows how to apply eyeshadow, whereas I never would.

"I'm only letting you do this because I'm going to miss you while you're in London," I say. "Are you packed yet?"

"Good question. Close your eyes."

I do, and let her smudge who-knows-what on my eyelids while she chats, "… and three pairs of jeans; two skinny, and that one low-rise pair, you know – now open your eyes for a minute – how cold do you really think it's going to be there? Do you think I'll need more than two cardigans …?"

While she talks, my mind slips away. Past this uncomfortable dress, and too-high heels, straight to the barn, where I wish I was instead. To where Jared should be right about now; dropping off the trailer, so we can load Jessie into it tomorrow morning, and take the mare back to the island with us tomorrow. The *island*.

Slate stops talking and leans back. "Hold out your hands. Nail polish."

"No. I hate it. It makes me feel claustrophobic."

"How can nail polish make you feel claustrophobic?"

"It's like my nails can't breathe when I have it on."

She stares at me, and I wave my non-polished hands. "I know, I know, nails don't breathe … I can't describe it; it's just a weird feeling. Plus, it's only going to start chipping off tomorrow and then it'll look worse than now."

She doesn't ask, or suggest, just states, "A light colour. You'll hardly notice. Just to show you've made an effort."

An effort. A glance at Slate's make-up mirror confirms how pink my cheeks are. Slate knows my bra is brand new, black lace, and that it matches my underwear. She knows how little time Jared and I have had alone this year. She knows I'll do a lot to impress Jared tonight.

I hold out my never-polished nails. "OK. Fine. Go."

"Oh Meggers, I'm so glad I didn't use any blusher on you; that natural pink in your cheeks is so cute."

"Yeah, well, it'll fade away when you're not around to embarrass me."

She laughs. "Oh, I'm sure Jared can bring a blush to your cheeks."

"Slate!"

Slate holds up the bottle. "Now, listen, you have to stay calm while I do this. Besides, Meg, it's natural to want tonight to be special. No more driving forty-five minutes to see Jared. No more dealing with college roommates there, and your parents here. That is definitely worth celebrating."

A rush of emotion dampens my mascaraed eyes. *Mustn't cry.* It's partly because Slate's right – I can't wait to be so close to Jared all summer – but also because of how well she knows me. How, despite the distance between us, she's listened to my worries all winter, and talked me through them.

"Thanks Slatey," I say. "You've been amazing this year. Remember what a mess I was when Jared first went to college?"

Slate rolls the nail polish bottle between her palms. "How could I forget? You were hyperventilating when you called. I asked if you crashed your car, or if someone died, and you said, 'No, Slate! Jared's residence is co-ed! The girls are funny, and friendly, and cute, and they're *there*; just down the hall!'" She pauses to unscrew the lid. "It took me half-an-hour to remind you, none of those girls were *you*. He loves you."

"Can you blame me for worrying, though? He's so …" A list of words to describe Jared runs through my head – thoughtful, generous, funny, loyal, determined – and I settle on "… perfect."

Slate swipes the tiny brush along my nail, leaving behind a strip of a pale, pearly colour I'm surprised I like. "Yup, and he feels the same way about you."

My hand finds the silver leaf pendant I've worn every day since Jared gave it to me at the end of last summer. "You're right. He's so good to me."

My phone rings. I lean forward and reach for it.

"No!" Slate slaps my hand away. "It'll ruin your polish."

"But, you're done!"

She shakes her head. "It needs to set. I'll answer it."

"Fine. It'll be Jared saying he's dropped the trailer off. You can talk to him, but no embarrassing me, or him. Not like last time when you asked him what his intentions were with me. Or like the time you …"

"Meg!" Slate taps my arm, and holds the phone out.

Her wide eyes worry me. "What?" I ask.

"It's Jared. You'd better take it."

***

I've been waiting so long for Jared's call with the good news that he's just half-an-hour away, that it takes me a minute to make sense of the bad news he's delivering. "It's Jessie. She's colicking. She's been down once, and it took three of us to get her back up."

Before I even end the call, Slate's packed my bag. She follows me down the stairs, and hands me my car keys. "By the time you get to the barn she'll be fine. You have everything you need in your bag; you can go straight to the cocktail party." She takes my face firmly between her hands, and looks me straight in the eyes. "Stay calm. Drive carefully. I'll lock up here. Go."

Normally, bombing down the highway with the twang of Gord Downie's voice on the stereo, the wind rushing through my hair, and a Diet Coke fizzing in my cupholder would have me singing out loud, grinning from ear-to-ear. Instead, the knot in my stomach just keeps tightening.

Jessie. I can't wait to see how she adapts to the island; see if it suits her as much as I think it will. What if I lose her before I can even get her there?

I glance at the speedometer. The last thing I need right now is a ticket. I ease off the pedal, watch the needle drop five km/h and make it a challenge. *See if you can hold it there 'till the next exit.* I calculate how long it will take to get from here to Jessie at this rate.

If I don't go crazy first.

***

Jared's waiting in the stable yard when I pull in. I'm so glad he hasn't changed for the dance yet. The familiarity of his worn jeans, and a once-black, sun-faded t-shirt, reassures me.

"Oh, Meg!" he says as soon as I step out of the car.

"What? Is she OK? Did something happen?"

Jared stands and stares. "She's fine. I mean, she's holding her own. Craig's walking her right now. But you ... I can't believe you."

"Oh." Of course. The dress. The too-short, too-shiny, maybe also too-clingy dress. And my heels. Which I meant to change at a stop light, somewhere along the way but, for once, the traffic gods were on my side, and I hit all greens.

My heels make us nearly the same height, which is what I notice when Jared steps forward, puts one arm around my waist, laces the fingers of his other hand through mine, and leans in so his breath warms my neck. "May I have this dance?" he asks. Little thrills pulse through my veins.

But Jessie.

"She'll be fine for two minutes." Can he read my mind?

My body says it first – melting into him, my dress slippery against his jeans, his fingers tracing circles on the bare skin on my back – so it's pretty much redundant when I whisper, "OK."

"I feel like I should be wearing a tuxedo to look half good enough to dance with you," he says.

"Well, I think you're perfect exactly the way you are."

***

Those two minutes of bliss, navigating puddles in the gravel of the yard, have to last us six more hours.

That's how long we walk Jess. And walk her, and walk her. That's how long it takes for her stomach to give an immense gurgle, and for her to cock her tail, and deliver the most beautiful pile of manure I've seen in my life.

On our way back to my house we pull into a McDonald's and carry two Big Mac meals to a high table in the corner.

"I'm so sorry, Meg," Jared says.

"About what? You were great. If it hadn't been for you checking in on her ..." My shudder is caused only partly by the over-active air conditioning.

"Your prom, you idiot." He reaches out, touches the still-clean bodice of my dress. The skirt's not looking as good; before I had a chance to change into my paddock boots, out of my heels, I took a bit of a tumble in the arena peat. "You missed it."

I shrug. Think of all the things I could say. Like how ever since Slate graduated, I have more acquaintances than friends at school. How I don't need to go to a hotel ballroom, and drink spiked punch, to make sure I'll stay in touch with my teammates from the cross-country team, and the group of us who edited the yearbook together. Like how, for me, this night signified moving forward, instead of looking back, and missing prom doesn't stop the forward movement.

"It doesn't matter. I'm happy," I say.

Jared blinks twice before nodding slowly.

I open my mouth to reassure him I really am fine. There will be other nights to dress up. Before I can speak, though, he smiles that lopsided grin I adore so much, and covers my hand with his. "You're amazing, Meg."

See? What else could I want?

Chapter Two

I don't know if it's the sun slanting through the gap in my curtains, Chester licking my hand, or my mom – coffee in hand – settling onto the edge of my bed that wakes me up, but I pop out of sleep humming.

"You're excited," my mom says.

"I am."

"Still not sad about the prom?"

"Still not sad ... except for the dress." I point at it, hanging on the back of my door, skirt crumpled and dirt-smeared. "It deserved better."

My mom squeezes my leg under the covers. "I'll drop it off at the dry cleaners on my way to work. They'll make it good as new."

"Thanks, Mom."

"It's easy for me to do, Meg."

"No, I mean thanks for letting me go back this summer. Thanks for letting me drive down with Jared. Thanks for ... trusting me, I guess."

She blinks. Sometimes I can literally see my mom struggling with her instinct to take control. She blinks again. "You've earned my trust. Both of you." She smiles. "It's been nice getting to know Jared this year. I really like him."

I grin. "I do, too. Speaking of which, do you know if he's up?"

She shakes her head. "I don't think so. You know he likes to sleep in when he stays here."

"Hmmm ..." I push upright, and swing my legs free of the sheets. "Time to get him up then, I think." I snap my fingers. "Come on Chester; let's go get Jared!"

The dog runs down the hall ahead of me, his nails scrabbling on the hardwood floor as he heads for the spare room door. Jared won't be asleep for long. Which is fine with me.

It's time to start our summer.

***

Jared's uncle, Rod, finds us on the ferry, sitting in the back of Jared's truck, overloaded subs dropping pickles and hot peppers onto the waxed paper spread in our laps.

"How are you two?" Rod asks.

I'm helpless, chewing, can only manage a "Mmm." Jared saves me, swallowing and saying, "Yeah, fine. Good. You?"

"Grateful, I guess." Rod looks at me. "Lacey is just loving Salem. And she's over the moon about working with you again this summer. She has big plans."

"Well, she wouldn't be Lacey if she didn't." I ball up the wrapper in my lap and stand, brushing crumbs from my shorts. "You want to see my new mare?"

"Sure."

Jessie's on the driver's side of the trailer. I open the top half of the escape door, and she pokes her head out. I stroke her dark moleskinned muzzle, brightening to an overall fiery chestnut red, with just a dab of white between her eyes, like someone smudged a thumb dipped in white paint there. Her nostrils flare, find my scent, and she whickers for the reward she hopes I'll have. I palm her a small chunk of carrot.

"I fell in love with her the first time I saw her," I tell Rod. "Which, I guess, is rare for her since she sprained one rider's ankle, and cracked another one's shoulder when she ran away with them."

"And you like her, why?"

I shrug. "I didn't know any of that the first time I got on her. I just rode her the way I like to ride, and it worked for her. I didn't expect her to panic, or run away, and she didn't." I straighten her forelock. "Plus, she teaches me something new every day."

Carrot swallowed, Jessie reaches out and lips at my hand, then my arm, working her way up to my neck. I giggle. "I guess it's one of those things. She's meant for me, and I'm meant for her. We love each other."

Rod smiles. "Well, Lacey's dying to learn more from you. She still has school, though, till the end of next week."

"I need to get settled, too. Wednesday will still be my day off, so once Lacey's done school, if that works for her, we'll set up a time for me to come out to your place."

Rod goes back to his truck, the ferry noses into the dock, and Jared and I roll through the village, with sweet Jessie behind us.

I can't wait to turn her out at Jared's. Can't wait to hack her in the fields. Can't wait to swim her in the river.

"It's so good to be home," I say.

Jared turns to me. "Yeah?"

My heart is full of something light – like helium – and I'm sitting in a beam of sunlight. I smile and nod. "With you. Just like before."

He smiles, but mostly with his mouth, and there's that funny double-blink again; the one from McDonald's. I'm imagining things, though, because he takes one hand off the wheel and uses it to tap my leg, just above my knee. "There's no way you're as happy as I am," he says.

***

The wind gusts through the window screen, and carries with it the rolling crunch of tires on gravel. I glance out the window. "Jared!"

I dump the still-folded sheets on the bare mattress pad of my bed and race to be out the front door before he can make it there.

"I didn't expect to see you so soon! I'm not even finished unpacking. Did you already fix that fence you were going to work on?"

This is what I missed during the school year. The way that, when we're on the island, Jared and I can just see each other whenever we feel like it. Last summer, for the first couple of months I knew Jared, I didn't even have his cell phone number – I didn't need it.

"The fence can wait a bit longer. I wanted to check on you."

"Well, I have enough food for the next few days, and my clothes are mostly in drawers. I still have to make the bed, but …"

Jared reaches out, takes my hand, and it silences me. We're not generally hand-holders. More shoulder-bumpers and knee-knockers. I look at his hand holding mine, then back at his serious face. "What?"

"We have to talk."

"Jessie?"

He shakes his head. "She's fine."

I had to ask, but I was sure it wasn't her. When I turned her out at Jared's, I slipped her halter off, and she nudged me good-bye the way she always does, then put her nose to the ground, and set off at a fast walk, then a trot, discovering the lush grass Salem liked so much last year; exploring the generous boundaries of her new field.

The buoyancy that's swelled my ribs and bounced my step all day is gone. The worry I carried for months; the anxiety I fought when Jared was away at college, rushes back, fast and familiar. "I knew I was too happy."

I watch Jared's face, willing that familiar smile to spread across his face – the one that pushes crinkles into the corners of his lips and eyes; the one that always chases my fear, worry, and sadness away. It doesn't come, though. His mouth is grim, and his eyes have none of their usual sparkle as he says, "How do you know it's something bad?"

"Because I'm not stupid."

He smiles, but it doesn't reach his eyes. My stomach drops.

"No, you're definitely not stupid," Jared says.

"So, what?"

"Do you want to sit down?"

There are chairs at the end of the porch, and countless seats inside, and a hammock between two big maple trees and, no, I don't want to sit in any of them. "No, Jared! I want you to say whatever you need to say, that I now clearly know is something not-good."

I don't know what I expected. Maybe that he needed to take back Jessie's field to graze cattle, or that the guy who loaned us the horse trailer for the summer wanted it back, or his mom said this summer we'd have to buy our own groceries, and stop raiding her fridge.

He squeezes my hand; crushing my fingers against each other. "I kissed someone else."

Holy shit. Holy hell. I can't breathe. My knees buckle. I should have sat down.

Jared reaches out with the hand not holding mine to steady me. "No!" I recoil, whip my hand free, step back, and back again. The stairs are beside me, and I stumble down, grip my stomach and crouch by the huge, showy hydrangea I've always hated.

I'm fighting for breath, wishing I could throw up, and propel this sick feeling out of me. But it's not going to be that easy.

Even though I know I'm not going to be sick, I don't straighten either. If I don't stand up, I don't have to look at him.

All my worries when he went to college – I wasn't crazy – I was right. I was right when I phoned Slate in a panic. I was right to have trouble sleeping.

Why did I have to be right? Right now I'd give anything to have been wrong.

"Meg?"

I press my hand to my eyes, but shock's still holding the tears back. *I knew it.* I knew it, I knew it, I knew it. And I was so stupid. I just let it happen.

"Meg?"

An ant climbs over my toe. "I hear you."

"OK."

I straighten, an inch at a time.

How could I have stopped it, though?

I ache the way I do after a full-day show.

I had to trust him. If I didn't, then what kind of relationship did we have?

I ache like I did after the Winterman half-marathon I ran in February.

But he was so perfect. I knew someone else would see it. How could they not?

I'm as sore as I was the day after Craig made me demo rising-trot-no-stirrups during an all-day clinic.

It was his job to say no. I should have been able to trust him to do that.

My mind spins back, picking out highlights of the last few months:

To Valentine's Day, when Jared set out a picnic on the floor of his cramped residence room, and we ended up rolling around, kissing in the middle of the food, so that when I got home, I found a heart-shaped chocolate lodged in my bra.

To all the times I'd come out of the big double doors of my school at lunchtime to find Jared in his truck, waiting by the kerb, to take me out for a quick sub or burger before driving all the way back to college.

To when I was jangling with nerves before teaching my first lunging clinic ever, and Jared drove me, and sat in the sub-zero arena the whole time I taught and, when I was finished, picked me up, right there in the ring, and spun me around, and said, "That's my girlfriend!"

Were those things all lies? Are those memories ruined forever?

Jared's sitting on the top step so, now that I'm upright, our faces are level. It's the worst time I've ever met his eyes. "You should go," I say.

"I thought …"

"You thought what? What did you think Jared?"

"I thought we'd talk."

"Yeah, well, you don't get to decide." It's the first time, since I've met him, that I truly don't want Jared around.

I bite my lip. Hard. Clamp my hand over my mouth. Shake my head and point at his truck.

He steps forward, but instead of turning to the truck, he walks down the stairs and reaches for my arm.

The questions crowd in. The horrible, terrible questions that I already know won't do any good. I watched Slate go through this with her first boyfriend. The more she knew, the worse it got.

But now I understand her compulsion to ask.

I open my mouth. *When? Who? Where? Why?* all bump around in my brain and I can't get any of them out.

Instead, the tears come; rising, burning my eyes. I pull away from him, thump up the stairs, and bolt for the safety of the cottage door.

Inside, door slammed behind me, back firmly against it, the shakes hit me. Shakes and heaves and sobs, too. Of course he can hear me – all the windows are open, and he's right outside – but I can't hold back any longer.

I reach behind me, fumble for the deadbolt and shoot it.

Eventually, I'll stop crying. Eventually, he'll leave. Eventually, I'll figure out what to do next.

Chapter Three

There's a note on the floor beside me. I must have stepped over it a dozen times while I was moving my stuff in. I recognize Betsy's sweet, slanting handwriting: *Meg, please join us for dinner, or dessert, or just company, if you like. Or, if you're tired, we'll see you tomorrow.*

I've run out of tears for the moment, but reading it makes me hiccup, and balloons an ache under my breastbone.

Red-eyed, with sobs just below the surface, I can't go see Betsy and Carl – can't risk being seen by guests – but I also can't be alone anymore.

It sucks that Jared's the one I want to see most. Not the I-kissed-someone-else Jared; the one from before. The one who's gone now.

I roll onto my knees and stand up. Look at the clock on the microwave. Slate will be on her way to the airport right now. I can't kill her excitement. I'll tell her later. When she's there. When I'm calmer.

I'm going to call my mom.

I don't know if it's a good idea, but it's the only one I've got right now.

I'm going to have to walk to get cell reception, anyway. It's a sunny day, and on clear days the signals soar away into the sky. I have to walk toward Kingston until my phone connects. That'll give me time to change my mind.

Halfway up the driveway I have half a bar. At the gate, I have three. That should do.

I take a deep breath. Am I going to do this?

I select Mom, push "Send" and lean against the gatepost while the phone rings.

"Meg? Hi, are you settled in?"

She's never been gushing. She's not cuddly. But she's my mom. Her voice reaches deep inside me, and drags out some terrible sounds, and I hang onto the phone, and hold onto the gatepost, and cry until I can speak.

"Meg, are you OK? Are you hurt?"

"No." I take a deep, shuddering breath. "It's not that."

"Do you think you can tell me?"

"I ... Jared ... kissed ... cheated ... ooooh ..."

"Oh, Meg. I'm coming."

"Y-y-y-ou c-c-can't."

"Yes I can. Why can't I?"

"Dad's p-p-party."

"Julianne Storm is an uptight snob. I've never liked her, and I don't want to go to her party. The Storms are your dad's clients and he can go." Her voice muffles, and I concentrate on my breathing – slowing it; calming it – while she murmurs to my dad in the background. Then she's back on the line. "If it's not too busy, I'll be on the eight o'clock boat. The nine at the latest. I'll bring food."

"Are you ..."

"I'm sure. I've decided. Now, Meg, do you think you can talk to Betsy?"

I shake my head. Remember I have to speak. "No."

"Alright. Listen, I know this is hard. I know it's terrible. I'll be there as soon as I can. In the meantime please just try to stay calm, and go to Betsy if you need to."

"'Kay."

"You'll take care of yourself?"

"Yes."

"This isn't the time to make decisions, or try to fix things. Just sit tight."

"OK."

It feels so weird to have just had that conversation with my mom, and to be standing here, under the blue sky, with the fluffy white clouds overhead, and swallows swooping all around me, with my life turned upside down.

This isn't the time to make decisions. Just sit tight.

She's right.

But I don't care. I shove my phone in my back pocket and, instead of heading back down the driveway to the cottage, I turn the other way. Onto the road. Toward Jared's.

I've run this route a hundred times, and ninety-nine times I've been happy doing it.

I really shouldn't be doing this. I'm not wearing my running shoes; I'm going to get shin splints.

Who cares?

Who cares takes care of a whole lot of niggling bits of common sense. Like, maybe this isn't the right time. And maybe I should listen to my mother. And maybe Jared and I need a while to cool off.

Who cares? Who cares? Who cares?

When I get to his driveway, he's disappearing into the barn, pushing the wheelbarrow, and I can't imagine anything that could make me angrier.

How *dare* he just get on with barn chores, like he didn't just wreck everything? Like he isn't a lying, cheating, asshole?

"Hey *jerk*!"

It's juvenile, but the release of yelling it from the barn door is worth it.

He drops the handles and turns to me. "Meg …"

"Shut up." The words don't release the tension fast enough. It just keeps building stronger and more insistent.

"I'm sorry," he says.

"And I'm angry. I *hate* you."

"Please don't …"

"What did you do, Jared? What does that mean – 'I kissed someone else' – I mean, that doesn't just happen. It's not just a kiss."

He stares at me, and his mouth twitches.

The bottom drops further out of my stomach. "Oh, God. I am so stupid. It wasn't just a kiss, was it? What was it – a date? Did you plan it ahead of time? Did you ask her out? Did you sleep with her?" I wrap my arms around my waist, bend over. "Oh, God, oh, God, oh, God …"

When I finally look at him, his eyes are red. "Do you actually want to know, Meg?"

"I actually wish I didn't *have* to know."

I turn away, then turn back again. "Was she from school?"

He nods.

"I *supported* you to go there. I had your back."

"I know. I'm ..."

"I *knew* this was going to happen."

His eyes open wide, and he blinks. "What do you mean? How could you know?"

"Look at you! Look how amazing you are ... were. When I met you I couldn't believe you were single. I knew some girl would hit on you at school. I knew it." The tears are running down my cheeks now. "But I didn't want to be *that* girl. That high school girlfriend who was jealous, and clingy, and insecure, so I told myself to be happy for you. But I was *right*."

Jared shifts his weight, and crosses his arms across his chest. "I can't believe you'd say that, Meg. Like it was inevitable ..."

"It was! You stupid, stupid, idiot. *You did it*. It happened. It's not like you can deny it."

"But ... but ..."

"Oh, shut up. Were you drunk?"

He lifts a hand to his forehead, runs his fingers through his hair. "We'd been drinking. At a party."

"*We*? You make me sick. I thought you and I were 'we.'"

"It wasn't serious. It wasn't *anything*. I didn't leave with her."

"Who is she?"

"Meg ..."

"Tell me! Who is she?" I don't know why it's so important to know. Maybe it's just that, compared to "why?" "who?" is more straightforward. A one-word answer.

And, also, it will tell me how mortified I need to be. I can't stand it if it was one of his college roommates I became friends with: sweet Pam, who loaned me her sweatpants when one of Jared's buddies spilled a beer on my jeans, or Hannah, who always included me in the college social events as one of "the girls" even though I was still in high school, or Raina – please don't let it be Raina – it always freaked me out how pretty that girl was …

"She's no one. She's nobody. She was finishing her program. I didn't see her again. She graduated, and she's moved to Alberta. It was a huge mistake." There's a shake in his voice that would spark my sympathy, if I wasn't so hurt myself.

I hate Jared's college. I hate every girl who graduated from it this year. I hate Alberta.

"Did I know her? Did I meet her?"

"No."

"No? You don't sound sure."

"No! OK, no! Is that sure enough? You never met her."

"If that's true, then what's her name? If I don't know her, you can tell me that."

"Meg …"

"Jared, you're not in a bargaining position right now. I. Want. To. Know. Her. Name."

"Fine. Fiona. Her name's Fiona."

Fiona.

My pulse drops a notch, breathing calms. He's right. I don't know a Fiona. I don't know why that makes it better, but it does. Marginally.

Until he makes the mistake of opening his big mouth. "Does that make it better? Or worse?"

My anger rears again. "You don't get to ask that! I'll be as angry as I want, for as long as I want, and you don't get to control it by throwing me a *name*." There's a bucket next to me, and I kick it across the floor. It's satisfying, so I pick up the broom and hurl it, too. In the background, Rex whines and slinks into a stall. I close my hands into fists, jam them by my sides and shake. "Now, I want to know *why*."

A tear spills down Jared's cheek. For a tiny moment I picture him crying in my car the day I took him to the dentist; the day leaving the island stirred up all his memories of his dad's death. There's a chink in my anger that lets in a wave of sadness. What a *waste*. I knew him so well. I loved him. Now all that's lost.

He clenches his fists, looks away, then back at me.

"It's the stupidest thing."

"Well it's not like you have any dignity left, so you might as well spill it."

He whispers, "I was jealous."

I'm hit with a fresh surge of fury so strong it catches my breath. "*You* were jealous? What did you have to be jealous of?"

His eyes flick back and forth – meeting mine, then looking at the floor – "You called me with all your university acceptances. Big schools, all over the place. Scholarships. That fancy program in Halifax. You were excited, and I thought 'That's it. She's going. I'll lose her.'" Finally his eyes rest on mine. "I was that guy – that jealous, clingy, college boyfriend. I was scared shitless."

"Oh my God. That is the stupidest thing I've ever heard. You were afraid of losing me, so you made sure you did? Nice move, Jared. Way to ruin everything."

Even as I'm saying this, the timeline registers. *My university acceptances* ...

The fresh shock cuts off the path between my brain and my mouth. "I ... I ..." I clap my hand to my chest.

Jared steps toward me. "What Meg? You look sick."

Like a gear catching, suddenly the words I need are there. "That was *weeks* ago, Jared. *Months*, even. So, am I sick? Yeah. You bet I am." When he first told me I wondered if all my memories were lies. Now it seems like all the recent ones are.

Jared's the one who looks sick now. "I tried to tell you. There was no good time. It was the hardest thing ..."

I clench my fists at my side, lean forward, and spit out my words. "Spare me! Spare me from the torture of having to listen to how hard this has been for you."

The rumble of a car engine drifts on the quiet evening air. My throat constricts. "I can't see your mom now."

I picture Jane's smiling face. So much like Jared's. Guarantee she'd ask me in for a delicious dinner; homemade macaroni and cheese, or chicken pot pie. The losses are bigger than me and Jared, and they're piling up already.

I turn around, and I don't look back. Jessie's by the fence, and I detour over to her, cup her muzzle in my hands when she reaches it to me. "I'll figure something out for you, girl."

Then I jog down the driveway so I'll be out of the way before Jared's mom turns in.

Chapter Four

My mom holds out a foot-long sub.

"I'm not hungry. I can't eat."

The wrapper's translucent with dressing.

"I had a sub for lunch."

But lunch happened in my old life.

A pickle peeks out, and I pop it in my mouth. "Mmm ..." Salty. Crunchy.

I pick up a soggy half of the sub. Take another salty, crunchy, bite. "You got extra pickles for me."

My mom points at a pickle falling out of her own sub. "Is there any point getting a sub without them?"

I eat the whole thing, then I lick my fingers, then – rather disgustingly, but it's not like I'm trying to impress anyone – lick the wrapper, too. I fold it into smaller, and smaller, even squares, then look at my mom. "Well, if I can eat like that I guess I'm not going to die."

"I'm glad."

"Thanks for coming," I say.

"My pleasure. Do you want to talk?"

"No. Yes. No."

"I get it."

I get up to fill the kettle so I don't have to look at her. "I went to see him. After I called you. When you said to sit tight. I hung up the phone and went and yelled at him."

I still have my back to her, but there's a hint of amusement in her voice. "Did it feel good?"

I flick the switch on the kettle, and turn to face her. "The yelling part felt kind of good. Other parts not so much."

"Like?"

"Like when he told me he did it because he felt jealous, or insecure, or something, about me getting all my university acceptances."

My mom's drumming her fingers on the table, but she has what I think of as her lawyer face on. Calm, waiting, listening. "And, how did that make you feel?"

"Pissed off. At the time. I told him it was pathetic. But now I wonder – did I tell him the wrong way? I thought I was excited, but was I gloating? Not that it makes what he did OK, but …"

My mom interrupts. "How did you feel when he told you he was going to college?"

"Happy for him, of course."

She waits, taps her fingers some more.

"And kind of insecure, and worried, and maybe jealous."

"And did you go out to a party and make out with some guy to feel better?"

"Uh, *no*."

"So is this your fault?"

The kettle thunks off. The tea bags swish as the hot water sweeps through them. I hand my mom her mug. "Point taken. Thanks."

I wrap my hands around the warmth of my mug. "I think I'm going to take this up to bed."

"Of course." My mom pulls out her laptop, fans papers on the dining room table, and dots the whole arrangement with a couple of highlighters.

I walk behind her chair on my way to the stairs and she reaches back, and trails fingers along my arm. She's not physically affectionate, but she's *here*. That counts.

Halfway up the stairs I look down at my mom's head bent over her notes. I ate a sub, and my mom's working; the world hasn't ended. Nothing's died but a silly teen relationship. I'll be fine after I've had some sleep. *Yup, just keep telling myself that ...*

I go to bed, and stare at the walls, and start the inevitable replay. What Jared said. What he meant by it. How I reacted. What I should have said if I was smarter, and quicker, and less stunned.

It doesn't take long until the tears are running down my face; soaking my pillow and pooling in the back of my nose to clog my breathing.

The stairs crack as my mom climbs them. The floorboards creak as she crosses them. My bed dips when she sits on the edge, and I finally fall asleep to the circling of her hand on my back.

***

In the morning I don't run, because I need a running route that doesn't go by Jared's.

But I swim, and wash my hair in the river, and scrub away the tightness on my skin from all the tears that dried on it last night, and when I come back in, my mom's slicing a grapefruit.

"Are you going to work?" she says.

I nod. "It's my first day. They're counting on me."

My mom pours juice into two glasses. "I think ..."

"You think what?" I prompt.

She sighs. "I don't know. I guess I think you shouldn't have to work if you don't want to, and you should work if you think it'll help."

"You would."

"Yep. I would. But I'm not always right."

"Well, I'm going to go, and do my best, and see."

"Are you going to tell Betsy and Carl?"

"I'll have to soon. But only when I think I won't cry. Or, at least, not in front of the guests."

I sip the juice she poured, and wince at the sharpness of the grapefruit. "I guess you have to go back soon?" It's hard to keep my voice neutral. Not to sound like I'm desperate for her to stay, and also not like I wish she'd leave. But it's a legitimate question. My mom rarely does planned vacations; never unplanned.

"I told Marcus I was going to work from here this week. I might go to a client meeting in Toronto at the end of the week. Depending ... but, other than that, I'm here."

"Well. Wow. Thanks."

I head up to work knowing the clock's ticking on when I'm going to have to tell Betsy and Carl what's up. My mom's presence for an entire week is going to be a big tip-off something's not right.

"Honey! So good to see you!" Betsy grabs me the minute I step through the door. "You didn't come up last night."

"Actually, my mom's here, working from the cottage while I get settled."

"We did see her car. Is everything OK? Are you sure you want to start today?"

"Absolutely!" I smile hard to push down the wobble in my voice that comes from the kindness in Betsy's voice; the concern raising her eyebrows.

All around me are bathrooms to clean, beds to make, and laundry to be washed and folded. Mindless, busy work that I want to be doing.

I have one of the most productive days of my life. Mental images of Jared kissing an unknown but, of course, gorgeous, stranger prompt me to pull out the vacuum. *When, how, where,* and *why* motivate a complete scrubbing of the refrigerator crispers. And, just to show I'm fine – *FINE* – each guest gets an extra-wide smile.

"Let me take these." I heft both the bags of the honeymooning couple checking in. "Please tell me more," I say to the white-haired man, binoculars slung around his neck, who's already given me a feather-by-feather description of seven of the birds he spotted today.

When everything's clean, and the guests are sipping fresh lemonade on the back patio, Betsy pulls out her apron. "Meg, I'm going to do some baking. Before you go, can you check the henhouse for fresh eggs?"

"Sure!" I love the light filtering through the cracks in the henhouse, and the cooing of the hens inside, and the warmth of their bodies, and of the eggs when I pull them out. My happiness at finding six fresh eggs is pure and uncomplicated.

Until I step out, and see Jared standing there. It's like walking into a brick wall and getting the breath, wind, *joy* knocked out of me.

"Meg."

"What are you doing here?"

"I had to see you."

"This is my *work*, Jared. My *job*."

"Well, I can't go to the cottage. I saw your mom's car there. She'd kill me."

"With good reason."

"I was afraid you wouldn't come up this afternoon ..."

"I won't. I'm not. You're going to have to look after Jessie for a couple of days."

"Of course I will, but Meg ..."

"What, Jared?"

"You just have to know how much I love you, and how sorry I am. I'd do anything ..."

I'm finding it hard to breathe. "Then don't upset me at work." Before he can step away I whip his cap off and nestle the eggs in it, then hand it back to him. "And Betsy needs these. You can take them in and tell her I had to go. I'll see her tomorrow."

"Meg. I can't."

"Yeah, well that makes two of us."

By the time I get to the cottage, the wind's dried my tears, and I'm left with an empty feeling inside.

My mom stretches out of her chair. "How did it go? Is there anything I can do for you?"

I nod. "You can call Rod and find out how much he'd charge for board. I need to find a new place to keep Jessie."

Chapter Five

By Wednesday, I've worked three solid days, and the only time I cried was when the chain of the leaf necklace Jared gave me last year broke; dropping the pretty pendant into the sink of the bathroom I was cleaning.

It was OK, though. I rinsed the tears away down the drain, and, back at the cottage, popped the silver leaf and broken chain into a shallow dish on the kitchen windowsill. I'll deal with it when I'm calmer.

My mom's filled the cottage cupboards and freezer with food, and arranged for Rod to board Jessie and, probably most importantly, helped me to sleep every night by patting my back.

It's easier to talk to her in those moments than it ever has been before in my life. Maybe because I'm staring at the wall, and don't have to worry about eye contact. Maybe because I don't have anything to lose.

"Has anything like this ever happened to you?" I ask.

She changes the direction of the circles she's doing on my back. "Nobody's story is exactly the same, Meg, but something like this has happened to most people. Something that hurts this much anyway."

"But you?"

"Sure, of course."

"Did Dad do it?"

"No. Not your dad."

I'm glad my dad never hurt my mom like this, but it might have been more reassuring to hear that he did, and they recovered from it.

My mom's mind gets there quickly. "He wasn't worth it – the person who hurt me like this. It wasn't like he was a nice person who made one mistake. There were lots of reasons we weren't right for each other."

She continues, "Without going into too many details, because there's only so much a girl should know about her mom and dad, there have been times when your dad's made me really angry, and vice versa, and we've worked it out. With the right person it's possible to get over big things."

I shift, pull my pillow tighter under my neck. "How do I know if we can get over it? How do I know if he's the right person? How do you decide to forgive somebody?"

My mom sighs. "I'm afraid I have a not-very-useful answer. I think you only know eventually. I think it's too soon to know right now, when it's all fresh. I hate telling you that, because what I'm saying is that you have to live with this feeling for a while, but I do believe it's true." She pauses. "Sorry."

I close my eyes, and my words come out in a sleepy, pillow-muffled mumble. "S'not your fault."

Jared comes to the cottage once, and my mom takes care of that, too. She steps out on the porch, and lets the screen door swing shut behind her while I hide around the corner. She's nice. Nicer to him than I was, but firm. "She's not ready to see you Jared." And then the thing that clenches my heart and wrings it out, is her voice dropping, and a creak as one of them takes a step – her toward him, I guess – and her words, "Oh, honey. I know it's hard. It's hard on everyone, but there's no quick answer."

That visit sends me sobbing to bed pretty quickly.

I've mapped out a new running route that doesn't pass by Jared's so, as soon as I move Jessie to Rod's, I should be good to get on with my new, different, summer.

I guess if everything in life truly does have a silver lining, the silver lining for me is learning I love the island no matter what. I could go home with my mom. Could take Jessie back to Craig's. After the success of my lunging workshop, and the other horsemanship workshops I've done for him, Craig would probably give me all the work I'd need this summer.

But I don't want to go. Even the prospect of facing the summer without Jared doesn't make me want to leave here. This island feels like home, and Betsy and Carl, and Lacey, and the other islanders I know, are like an extended family.

I'm not giving that up because of Jared.

Today – my day off – is the day we're moving Jessie. I want it done in the morning. After Jared goes out in the fields to work, and well before Lacey's home from school. I'll talk to her soon, but not today. First Betsy and Carl, then Lacey. As soon as I'm ready.

We drive Carl's borrowed truck to Jared's, and I don't look at anything but the trailer, sitting empty right where we left it just a few days ago. I concentrate on backing the truck up, straight and true, until my mom's raised hand tells me I've got the hitch lined up with the coupler, and then I do all the things I've watched Craig, and Jared, and a hundred other horse people do, a hundred other times.

I test the lights six times, just like Jared always does, and then I take a deep breath. "I guess I'll just go get her."

Jessie trots to me, nickering, and I press my face against her neck, and breathe the smell I know so well. Priorities. I've got to keep them straight. Her being safe and happy is number one. I know she's been safe here, with Jared – know that for sure – that she'd always be safe with him. But I can't come here to ride her, so she's got to move.

"Come on, angel." Jessie's got her sensitivities, but loading isn't one of them. She clomps up the ramp, knowing there's a haynet inside, and before long I'm easing out of park, taking the turn out of the driveway wide and slow, and trying not to look in the rearview mirror.

If Jessie's relaxed ears and bright eyes are any indication, her ride over was fine, and she unloads easily into Rod's yard. Salem comes to the gate, and my heart lifts to see her. I graze Jessie outside the paddock for a bit, while Salem grazes inside, and then I take her into the fenced-in sand ring.

My mom's brought her laptop, and she leans against a tree, tapping at the keyboard, while I free lunge Jessie. She's always stiff, and the vet, farrier, and chiropractor combined have never been able to figure out why. It's one of the reasons Craig signed her over to me in exchange for the horsemanship lessons I taught every Saturday all winter for him. Because I don't want to show her, I don't care if she's stiff to start out with. Most days she works it out, and some days she doesn't. On those days I don't ride her. For me, it's simple, and easy.

"Tuh-rot!" I ask, and she does; not perfectly smoothly, but not bad for a few days with no exercise.

As she trots, her gait smooths, her neck arches, and her ears swivel ahead, to me, to Salem, and behind her. The sun glints off her fine, red, coat and a breeze lifts her mane.

"You look happy." My mom's leaning on the sand ring fence.

I shrug. "She's happy, and I'm responsible for her, so I'm happy."

My mom nods. "I know how that feels."

We finish with a couple of rounds of canter both ways, and I'm letting Jessie walk out when Rod pulls in.

My mom walks to meet him, then they both come to me.

"So, this is the mare who's going to keep Salem company?"

I nod. "Eventually. If it's OK with you, I'll turn her out in the sand ring, with some hay, for the first couple of days; so they can be close to each other, but still have some space. Then I'll move her into Salem's paddock."

He shrugs. "You're the expert. Whatever you want is fine with me."

I pat Jessie's neck and slip her a carrot. "Good girl. You're done." Then I step out of the ring to stand in front of Rod.

"Listen Rod, I really appreciate this. You're doing me a big favour. I'll come by later and talk to Lacey about it, and we'll make sure the work comes out fairly."

He adjusts his cap against the nearly-noon sun. "Meg, I can't think of anything that would make Lacey happier than having you and your mare here. I'm sorry you've had to move her, but we're happy to have her."

As we drive home with the empty trailer rattling behind us, my mom clears her throat. "Do you think he *knows*? What happened, I mean. Why you're moving Jessie from Jared's."

I sigh. "I don't know, Mom. I'm not even sure what Jared will tell his mom. I mean, it's an awkward thing to have to explain ..." I roll my shoulders back and lift my chin. "The one thing I know for sure is I have to be above it. It's a small place, and there will be rumours, but I just have to treat people the way I normally would. Starting with Rod."

"He seems like a nice man."

"He *is* a nice man. They're all nice in that family." I grip the steering wheel until my knuckles turn white, and bite my lips, then turn to her. "That's what makes this so hard."

***

My mom's scrolling through messages on her phone when I pull into Jared's driveway. "Do you need help?" she says.

"Nah, I can do it." I *can* do it. I'm OK on my own.

She props her elbow on the open passenger window. "Just call me if you need a hand."

I don't, though. Unhitching is even easier than hitching. A tiny bubble of pride swells my chest. I have everything uncoupled, and the trailer jacked up, clear of the hitching ball, when I hear Jared's voice. "Hey!"

I straighten, and shade my eyes. He's striding out of the barn. "Yes?" I say.

"What are you doing?"

"Returning the trailer. We borrowed it from Steve together, so I figured it was OK for me to use it. It's back, fine. Nothing happened to it."

"You took her?"

"Jessie? Yeah. She's my horse."

"I can't believe you just took her without saying anything. I liked her. I've been looking after her."

The breeze blows hair across my face, and I pull it back again. "Well, I'm sorry if it hurts your feelings. That's what happens when people break up, Jared. It *hurts*. In lots of ways."

He flings his arms out. "Break up? So now we're broken up?"

It feels like everything behind my breastbone crumples. Like all my insides are squished and aching. No way. This is not fair. *He* cheated on me and *I'm* the one who has to give the break up speech?

"What else could we be, Jared? What did you think would happen? Everything's different now."

"I know, Meg. If I could take it back I would. But I can't. And I *told* you. Doesn't that count for anything? I told you because I love you. Because I want to work things out."

"That's fine for you, Jared. You've had time to think about this; to get used to it, and decide we can work things out. You've been lying to me for so long. But I *just* found out."

I shake my head. "Believe me, I hate this. I wish I could forget about it. I wish we could just work it out. But I don't even know how I'm going to feel next week, or tomorrow, or an hour from now. I'm just getting by minute-by-minute right now ..."

That's it. I can't say anything more. I walk back to the driver's side of Carl's truck. It takes all my restraint not to gun the engine – I need to roll slowly away just in case I forgot to unhook something – I'm biting my lip as I ease my foot onto the gas.

I glance over at my mom, and her phone's in her lap, she's staring straight ahead, and there are tears brimming in her eyes.

Like I said, there's lots of hurt to go around.

Chapter Six

Thursday morning Betsy's deadheading geraniums when I get up to work. "Did you have a good day off? Did you and Jared take that horse of yours somewhere?"

I take a deep breath. I've got to get this done. I pick up a spent flower she's dropped, hold it out to her and *go*. "Betsy, Jared and I broke up."

She whirls on her heel, and her hand flies to her chest. "No!"

"I thought you might know already. You always know everything happening around here."

She's shaking her head. "No, no, no. Not you two." She looks at me. "I knew something was unusual – to have your mother here. And I guess I wondered why you needed to borrow Carl's truck instead of just using Jared's, but no … not this."

She pulls me into a hug. "It's silly to say this, but even with all the relationships I've seen come and go over the years, I didn't see this one ending."

She steps back. "I'm sorry. I suppose that doesn't make you feel much better."

"Don't worry about it. Nothing makes me feel very good these days, Betsy."

***

Now just to tell Lacey, and then I'll let island gossip do the rest. I drive out to ride Jessie after work, and find Lacey grazing the two mares together. "I hope it's OK Meg! I want them to get to know each other. I just love Jessie. She's beautiful."

Jessie's trademark laid back ears, swishing tail, and bared teeth are nowhere in sight. She's tearing at the deep grass, and seems to feel like the six foot gap between her and Salem is an acceptable buffer. "Yeah, well, she's also known to be a bit intolerant of other horses. Although she looks good right now. You must have the touch."

"I'm so happy you brought her. We'll be able to ride together all the time. And there's something I want to ask you about ..."

"Lace, we need to talk."

"Oh?"

"Come on; do you want to try these two in the paddock together while we're here to watch?"

"Sure."

I open the gate, and Lacey leads them both through, then unclips the leads from their halters. Jessie instantly flattens her ears, and snakes her head toward Salem, only to encounter Salem doing exactly the same thing. My chestnut mare jerks her head back, and up, then wanders to a patch of grass and starts grazing.

I laugh. "She's used to being turned out with two young geldings who skitter ten feet away every time she bares her teeth. Salem might be good for her."

"So?" Lacey props her foot on the fence rail beside me. "What's up?"

Getting started is tough. Lacey's taller than last year – the two-inch gap between the bottom of her breeches and her ankles tells me that – but she's still a freckle-faced, curly-haired kid. She looks at me with wide eyes and raised eyebrows – like she'd listen to anything I said – like I have all the answers to the world's problems.

I wish.

I sigh. "Lacey, I'm really happy to have Jessie here, and to be able to see you, and Salem, all the time …"

She tilts her head to the side. "But?"

"But the reason I brought her is that Jared and I … aren't together anymore."

"What? What do you mean 'aren't together?' Of course you are. We all had Easter dinner together, and I saw you on the May long weekend. And you wear his …" She gasps, pats the empty area at the base of my neck. "His necklace …"

Her eyes widen even more. "Are you serious, Meg? You and Jared broke up?"

I was afraid her distress would send me into tears as well, but I'm unexpectedly calm. I nod.

"What happened? Did you break up with him? Why?"

"Oh, Lace. It's just … some things happened and we need to figure them out – we need to see if we can figure them out."

"So it's not forever?"

"I wish I knew, Lacey."

"Do you still love him?"

"Yes. Of course. If I didn't love him, this would be no big deal. Your cousin is one of the best people I've ever known in my life."

Now the tears are prickling my throat, and the inside of my nose. I brace myself for her next question.

It doesn't come. Instead she gives a very loud sniff. And then another.

I open my arms, and she walks into them, and throws her arms around me. "Oh Meg, I'm so sad." She hiccups, and pushes her cheek against my arm.

I hate that she's sad, but there's a weird relief in it, too. It means I'm not crazy for still crying myself to sleep. It means this break-up is a big deal to other people; not just to me.

Of course, it also means it's going to be super-hard to get through it.

***

The day my mom leaves, she comes up to have lunch with us at the B&B.

"It's been ages since we've seen you here for so long, Emily. It's been really nice."

"You know, Betsy, it's been nice to be here. I got a lot of work done, and I'm so relaxed."

Betsy shoos me out to say good-bye to my mom while she washes the dishes.

My mom's car is packed, she drove it up, and is leaving straight from here to catch the one-fifteen boat.

We both pause by the driver's door.

"So ..." I say, and "Well ..." she says.

Then she takes control of the conversation. "I'm worried about you, Meg." I open my mouth, and she holds up her hand. "Just let me say this. You're already doing better than I would have in your place – trailering horses around, and working hard for Betsy – but you're going through something tough. I'm afraid you'll be lonely."

I take a deep breath. "I might be. I will be – sometimes – but I'll be OK. I'll figure it out. And I've got Betsy and Carl, and Lacey, and Jessie on my side, so that's great."

"Maybe you could meet some new people? There are always activities going on in the village; maybe you could join something?"

I picture the hand-lettered signs advertising euchre nights that are always posted on the ferry cork board. There are usually notices for golf lessons, too. "Maybe." I nod, to make my words more convincing. "I'll look into it."

My mom brushes a few wind-blown strands of hair off my forehead. "You do that." Then, as though that one small touch was just a warm-up, she reaches out and hugs me to her. "Take care of Jessie, and take care of Betsy and Carl, and work hard – but not too hard – and take care of *you*."

"OK. I will." My voice is muffled against her shoulder. "You should come back."

"I will." She pulls away and drops into the car. "Call me every now and then. Keep me posted."

Constriction seizes my throat as her car bumps and rattles down the gravel driveway. But that's OK; I'm getting used to this edge-of-tears feeling.

Then, when I go back inside, and Betsy has a glass of lemonade and a slice of pie waiting for me, the tightness gives and I sniff, and cry, then wipe my eyes and tell her. "That's enough for now. No more crying for a while. Time to get on with my summer."

***

"You just come back up here if you're lonely tonight!" Betsy waves from the door as I leave work.

"I will." But I have no intention of going back. I have to exercise Jessie, and I need to leave right away if I want to cycle over there, ride her, and cycle back before dark.

Was it a good idea to move her to Lacey's? I imagine going up to Jared's instead, and my pulse races. I said I was moving on; getting over things. The ten kilometre cycle is just the price I have to pay to help me with that.

I have my foot raised to step onto the cottage porch when I stop. *What?*

Parked further back than we normally do, so it's behind a big lilac bush that grows by the driveway, is a car.

Mom? Jared? It's not anybody's car that I know. It's way too funky, and completely adorable; tiny and a bright, acidic, green.

"Hello? Is somebody here?" Nobody answers so I circle the cottage. "Hello? Anyone?"

I come back out beside the car, and now I can see a huge red bow on the steering wheel. I walk over and try the door. It's unlocked. I ease it open as though something might jump out at me; as though it's booby-trapped.

There's a sheet of paper on the driver's seat, with a set of keys lying on it. I pick it up.

Meg,

I think you made the right decision moving Jessie, but I also think you need a reliable way of getting there.

I hope having this makes your life easier this summer, and I hope you have a great summer.

I'm here if you need me.

Mom

Oh. My. God. I have a car?

I pick up the keys, and push the button on the keyfob. The car beeps. *My* car beeps.

I have a car. I have a car!

I whirl around, run back toward the path.

Oh! The door's open. I run back, push it shut, and, still gripping the keys, run back to the path. And run, and run, and run. When I burst onto the B&B lawn, I yell, "Betsy! Carl! I have a car! My mom left me a car!"

Betsy opens the door, laughing. "So, you like it?"

"You knew?"

"Of course I knew. I drove your mom to pick it up at the used car lot in Kingston. Why are you standing here yelling about it? Go and drive it up here."

"Oh. Of course. I will. I'll be right back …" And I belt back down the path to my new car.

***

On my way to Lacey's, Jared drives his familiar pick-up by without a second glance. I have to take a deep breath to get past my wrench at seeing him, out and about, getting on with life without me. Then I throw my shoulders back. I'm independent. I'm anonymous in the car nobody knows is mine yet. I can get on with my life too.

In fact, if she was here, Slate would tell me I'm better off without him. She'd make a list of all the bad things about Jared.

Problem is, the list would be pretty pathetic:

- He likes anchovies on his pizza. But he's always willing to order without them to make me happy.
- All his socks have holes in them. But his toes are cute, and I knew exactly what to put in his stocking at Christmas; a dozen pairs of sport socks.
- He listens to country music all the time. Well, I could never, in a million years, tell Slate this, but I have one or two country songs on my iPod now.

Jared's always been generous to me, and thoughtful. He calls when he says he will, and he's never late. He's stubborn sometimes, but so am I – it's a trait I can understand.

The only really truly terrible thing Jared has ever done is cheat on me, and break my heart, and that's what I'm trying to avoid thinking about right now.

I need my horse to help me with that.

It's Sunday night, so Lacey's family are over in Kingston having dinner at her grandmother's. Salem and Jessie are grazing – close enough that it seems possible they don't hate each other – far enough apart that I can give a carrot to each of them without the other pinning her ears.

I lead Jessie in to Lacey's snug little barn, and use the grooming mitt to scratch the itchy spot on her neck; smooth my softest brush over her silky coat. There's a nick on her rump which,

I bet, matches Salem's teeth. I'm not worried about it; this is Salem's turf, and Jessie needs to learn some manners.

In the sand ring I mount and let Jessie swing into her forward, reaching walk. We spend five minutes walking, both directions, reins at the buckle before, with the lightest contact gathered on the reins, I think 'trot' and she trots.

It's trademark Jessie; leaping forward, racing down the long side, until she notices I haven't grabbed at the reins, and I'm not rising quickly enough to match her pace, and she snorts, and slows, and I pick up the reins, and she stretches into them.

As always, there's a bit of stiffness to our first few times around the ring, but it's not bad today. In fact, it hasn't been bad for a long time now, ever since I started being the only one to ride her. Since I became willing to just back off and lunge her, and give her a massage, and turn her out when she's particularly stiff.

She always moves better after a canter so, again, I just think it, and she springs forward, nose nearly pressed into her chest, breath coming deep and ragged. Again, I refuse to get sucked into her panic; I don't grab at the reins; just lift my seat off her back, sink my weight in my heels, and wait until her breathing quiets, and she stretches forward for my contact.

And then we're in the zone.

This is the reward for dealing with the fiery attitude Jess always throws out during the first fifteen minutes of every ride.

Once she's accepted I'm in for the long haul – I'm not going to over-react to anything she does, and I want to move forward just as much as she does – she agrees to be my partner. She holds the bit carefully, pushes us both up, and forward, from her hind end, and gives me the kind of powerful, floaty ride that spoils me for other horses.

She's taught me so much, already, and she teaches me more every day, and that's why I don't need her to compete, and I don't even need her to be one hundred per cent sound every day, I just need her to trust me, and accept me.

"I'll always love you, and I'll always look after you," I tell her as I straighten her forelock, and rub her poll, and let her loose with Salem.

She stands at the gate and watches me walk away, and that's the other reason I love her so much. She's the most loyal horse I've ever known. She used to nicker for me from the field even before she was mine; even when I only rode her once a week. She'll bare her teeth at another horse walking by, but always turn back to me with a nuzzle and a bump.

Jess loves me, and my mom loves me, and Lacey loves me, and Betsy and Carl love me, and I'll be OK, even if I still really, really love somebody I can't have anymore.

My phone's fallen onto the driver's seat and I have to lift it out of the way when I get back in. Because of the dodgy reception at the cottage, my inbox usually fills up when I get closer to Kingston.

I scroll through five new messages.

My mom: Just checking in. Got home safely. Noticed sign for drop-in yoga classes in community hall Tuesday nights – might be worth trying!

Slate: Guys with British accents are hot. Best thing? They think girls with Canadian accents are hot.

And then three, from Jared, sent at different intervals. All saying the same thing. Working together to send my pulse racing. **I'm sorry.**

I'm sorry, I'm sorry, I'm sorry.

Yeah? Well I'm angry, I'm angry, I'm angry.

Delete, delete, delete.

Chapter Seven

I wake up Wednesday morning with no work to distract me, no boyfriend to hang out with, and, this week, no mom to help fill the empty hours.

But I've still got a horse to ride, so I face my bike into the fierce island wind, and pedal to Lacey's. I love having the car, but today I want to keep busy and end up tired, so it's cycling for me.

Lacey comes out as soon as she sees me. I help her muck out the barn and scrub the water buckets, then we take the horses on a hack.

She talks about school, and how next year she'll have to take a bus off the island for Grade nine; "It'll be so weird to be gone every day."

I also find it hard to imagine Lacey going from the tiny village school, with a total of less than forty students, and Grades five through eight taught together, to a downtown high school in the city, with over a thousand students.

It'll change her – some of her goofy innocence is bound to be worn away. I know she has to grow up, but I'll miss the Lacey I love right now.

All the more reason to enjoy hanging out with her this summer.

Lacey tells me Salem's been great. "But we both have a few bad habits, so maybe you can help us?"

She asks about Jessie, and I tell her about my long days at Craig's barn; teaching grooming, and tacking up, and parts of the horse, to his beginner students before and after they rode, and about how Jessie would follow me up and down the fences when I was walking other horses, and how she pressed her face against my back when I was standing in the aisle talking to six little girls about how to wrap bandages.

"She wasn't that way with everyone. It made me feel special. I guess we just clicked, and the rest is history."

Lacey opens her mouth and, for a minute, I'm terrified she's going to ask about Jared – about how we could have clicked so strongly last summer and how we've unclicked now.

But that's not it. "Since you were teaching groups all winter, do you think you'd teach some of my friends this summer? Would you be our coach?"

Coach? That's not me. More like a teaching assistant, at the most. If the barn was summer camp, I would have been a counsellor-in-training. I answer quickly. "I'm not a proper instructor, Lacey. I wasn't teaching riding, just horsemanship."

"That doesn't matter. I know you could do it. And we *really* need a coach. Do you remember my friend Bridget?"

Bridget. So familiar. Why am I associating fish and chips with Bridget's name?

I snap my fingers and Jessie's ears swivel to me. "The fish fry!" And then the reason for the fundraising fish fry floods in. "How is she? Is everything OK?"

We step out of the treed area we've been riding through and Lacey clucks Salem up to ride beside me. "Oh, she's great! She finished the chemo a while ago. She's starting to get fuzzy hair." Lacey brushes her hand across her velvety helmet.

"And that's the thing. Last year, when we first found out she was sick, we went to the Dixon fair and watched this musical ride competition they have there. Bridget loved it, and I told her we'd do it when she was better."

"That's a nice idea."

"Yeah, well we can't do it alone. We need a coach. We need you to help us." Lacey keeps talking while we cross the highway and ride onto her driveway. "I have Salem, of course, and Bridget has a horse the Children's Wish Foundation helped pay for – with some of the money from the fish fry. And our other friend, Carly, has a horse. I told them you'd be a great coach ..."

We halt in the yard, and I kick my feet out of the stirrups and slide off Jessie's back. "I don't know, Lace. It sounds like a lot of work. And a musical ride – would I have to choreograph it, too? I've never done anything like that."

Lacey completely ignores Salem, who's tearing at long grass despite still having her bit in. "You can do anything, Meg. You're so smart. I know you could. Please say yes!"

"I'd have to meet the others," I say. By which I kind of mean no.

"No problem. I'll set it up." By which, I have the feeling Lacey means 'It's a done deal.'

***

Even after all this, there's a good chunk of the day left ahead of me. Instead of heading back to the cottage, I cycle the opposite way, skirting the shore, staring over to Kingston, into the thick of the wind turbines.

I pass the tiny ferry to Ellicott Island, across the Navire Channel. Ride till I run out of paved road, and keep cycling on dirt road. I'm in a rhythm established by the swish-crunch of my tires through gravel, the rush of my own blood through my ears, when I hear another noise; a rustling and some snapping. I turn to see what's coming out of the bushes by the side of the road, and my heart nearly stops, then begins to thump double-time.

A bull.

Holy heck. The heft of his head, the breadth of his chest, take my breath away. My bike seems like a joke underneath me. Something he could trample and twist with no effort at all.

I look at him and he looks at me. *Keep pedaling.*

How will he react to a bike? *Keep pedaling.*

I'm past him now, and I glance back to see him coming up, and out, of the shallow drainage ditch by the side of the road. *Keep pedaling.*

He reaches the road, and the distance is widening between us, but another look behind me shows him swinging into a jerky trot. *Oh my God.*

How fast can he run? I have no idea. I just pedal, and pedal, and pedal. *Count to a hundred, don't look back. If you do he'll be right there.*

I count to a hundred, and then add fifty more. Concentrate on pushing down with my raised leg, pulling up with my lower one. Making each pedal stroke count.

When I reach the paved highway again, I slow and take a look. He's back quite a ways, no longer trotting. Still moving, but not close enough that I feel I could be his target.

The adrenaline I didn't know was driving me drains away all at once, and a strange tingling rushes all through my body, settling in my knees. I flag down an approaching pick-up. "There's a bull loose. Just back there." I point. The driver's not much older than Jared.

Wait 'till I tell Jared ...

I realize I won't. Not today. My chest tightens, and my vision blurs, but I stick to my promise – *no tears* – except the ones whipped out of the corners of my eyes by the island wind.

There's an empty ache in my gut, too, and, when it doesn't subside, I recognize it for what it is. Hunger. I'm completely starving. I need to stop in the village on my way home.

I could get a healthy cream cheese and cucumber sandwich on Red River bread fresh from the bakery, but instead I head into the general store for Cheetos and Diet Coke. Probably not one natural ingredient in my entire lunch.

There are benches at the Boat Club. I've always liked them. They're carved out of wide planks of someone's fallen tree and, flanking a massive oak that grows near the water, they look like they're part of the trunk. It's a perfect place to take my food.

Between ferries on a weekday, it's quiet everywhere in the village. But here, there's an extra layer of peace from the lapping of the waves, and the clinking and sighing of the breeze through sailboat rigging.

The blue shimmer of the water makes me wish I'd worn my bathing suit underneath my clothes. I finger-comb my hair; loosening it from around my ears, lifting it away from my forehead, where it's still damp from wearing a helmet during all that cycling.

I wander toward the wooden clapboard clubhouse that, when viewed from the road, tilts slightly. There's a recycling bin for my empty can, and notices posted in the window. **LEARN TO ROW!** Hmm ... a team sport. Not my forte. Which makes the Dragon Boat Fridays even less my thing.

SAILING LESSONS. I glance out at the river. All the way across to Kingston there are white sails. Some close by, others just triangles in the distance. My big brother Cam sails a lot. In fact, he spent last summer navigating the St. Lawrence on a fifty-foot yacht – jointly owned by the Biology department where he studies, and the Ministry of the Environment, and fitted out more like a floating lab than a pleasure craft.

Carl sails, slipping out in a tiny one-man dinghy whenever the winds are right and his mowing is done.

I've sailed too. Cam used to take me when he still lived at home. I liked it but, unlike Cam, didn't have a best friend with a sailboat I could use. And, of course, there was the whole horse-crazy thing.

"You live here?" I turn to face an older man, white haired with twinkling eyes. This guy could grow a beard and be a very convincing Santa Claus.

"Pardon me?"

"Sorry, young lady. My daughter says I need to work on my social skills. What I meant was, are you just visiting the island, or are you a potential customer?"

I laugh. "I'm spending the summer at my family's cottage on the south shore, next to Betsy and Carl Waitely's B&B. I work for them."

"Ah, Betsy Waitely ... or Carter, as I used to know her. Now that woman can bake a mean pie ... anyway, we're not here to talk about pies; we're here to find out when you can take sailing lessons."

"Oh, I don't know about that ..."

"You sailed before?"

"A long time ago. I was a kid."

"What did you like about it?"

His question fills my head with images. Sun dancing on waves. Cam grinning. Spray arcing through the air. "The wind. How strong it was. And sometimes quiet too. And how you couldn't rush."

He laughs. "So true. Time becomes less important when you're out there." He taps the glass, beside the "Sailing Lessons" notice. "Maybe you should try again."

I shake my head. "Those are all evenings and weekends. I can't really do those." I lift my arms, palms up. "This is my day off."

"Come along then."

"Pardon me?"

But he's already off, following flagstones embedded randomly in the grass; a sort of, kind of, half-path. The glass in the door of the Boat Club rattles, and the door knob jiggles as he grunts, gives it a push, and it jerks inward.

Oh, the summer smell of an old wooden house that's had sun beating down on it all day long. Rafters, and joists, and worn wood floors, all heated up and giving off a nearly musty scent – except cleaner – and somewhere in there is the whiff of old paint, too. And something else.

He leads me into a back room, walls covered with bags, hanging from hooks and nails banged right into the walls, and maybe this is it – the smell I can't quite identify – the sails and the ropes. The part of my brain that stores the scent of a barn, has held onto this too. For just a minute I'm eleven, and my big brother's by my side.

"Adam, I've got someone to meet you."

A guy – my age maybe – stands up from where he's crouched in the corner of the room, doing I'm-not-sure-what, to I-don't-know-what piece of sailing equipment.

He pushes blond hair – thick and sun-crisped – out of his face.

The atmosphere of this place has me smiling. Maybe that's why he smiles too.

He puts out his hand, and I look from his hand to his face. Other than occasionally meeting my parents' clients, the last time I shook hands was in Guides. And that was with my left hand. I put my right hand out to meet his, and his grip is dry and firm.

"Adam Turlington."

"Meg Traherne."

"Nice."

Nice what? Nice name? Nice handshake? Nice day?

It's nice to be nice. My extra-sweet kindergarten teacher, Mrs. Noakes, always used to say that. And she was right; it *is* nice to be nice, so I should give this guy a break.

Correction, I should give this *cute* guy a break.

Guilt flutters through me, and my hand flies to my breastbone. To finger my pendant. Which, of course, is gone. I trace a little circle on my skin instead.

So, he's cute? So, I noticed? If it brightens my day, so what?

It takes me a minute to register Santa Claus's words. "This young lady ... Meg ... would like to have sailing lessons. But they'll have to be private. Only on Wednesdays. You can do that, right?"

This is my chance to say no. But sailing lessons are definitely better than euchre, or golf. And yoga's never been my thing. And I wouldn't mind seeing Adam's smile once a week.

So, I don't protest.

"Sure," he says. "You'll have to come to my place, though."

Santa nods. "Good idea Adam. You can use the old Laser." He turns to me. "Ellicott Island. Can you get there?"

Since the turn-off for the ferry to Ellicott Island is just past Lacey's place, I'll be there to ride Jessie every Wednesday anyway. "Sure, yes. That's fine."

Adam nods. "Good. Nine a.m. next Wednesday? It'll be a nice way to start the day."

This guy seems to think a lot of things are nice.

That's fine. I can live with nice. Nice is relaxing. Nice is easy. Nice is a good antidote to gut-wrenching, tear-my-insides out angst.

It will be nice to have a nice Wednesday morning to look forward to.

Before I get back on my bike I text my mom.

At Boat Club. Just signed up for sailing lessons. Start next week.

Everything I've typed is true. It's not the meeting-new-friends, social-networking type of activity my mom had in mind, but she doesn't have to know that.

And I think it'll be fun.

Chapter Eight

I t's Saturday morning, and I'm stirring pancake batter, when two arms go around my waist and squeeze the breath from me. "Surprise!"

"Lace! You crazy girl! What are you doing here?" I say.

"Dad had to pick something up at the foot so I tagged along. I wanted to tell you I set up that meeting."

"What meeting, Lace?"

"You remember, Meg. That day on the hack; you said you'd meet with my friends. To start planning the musical ride."

"No, wait, Lacey. I didn't say we'd start planning it. I said …"

Betsy walks in with an armful of fresh rhubarb from the garden. "Good morning Lacey. To what do we owe the honour?"

"Meg's going to be my coach. Mine, and my friends. We're going to do the musical ride at the Dixon Fair in August. It's to celebrate Bridget being better, so Meg has to meet her."

Lacey turns to me. "Tonight. After work. Can you come? We want to meet at Bridget's."

I pour the first pancake onto the griddle. "I don't know, Lace. I don't even know where she lives …"

Betsy clears her throat. "I have to go by there tonight anyway. I can give you a lift if you like."

I raise my eyebrows. "Oh. Thanks. Betsy. Now I have no reason not to go."

Lacey grabs my arm and jumps up and down, making for one very wobbly pancake. "Oh, yay! Great!" She whirls to face Betsy. "By the way, what's Jared doing here?"

My stomach was grumbling – I was hungry for a spare pancake – but now my appetite's disappeared. "Jared?"

Betsy speaks quickly. "I meant to tell you, Meg. He offered to help Carl get that old fence along the road fixed up. He won't be anywhere near the house."

A horn beeps twice, and Lacey jumps. "That's my dad. I'd better go."

I hold the spatula out to Betsy. "Can you take over the pancakes while I walk Lacey out? I'll check for eggs while I'm there."

Lacey jumps in the truck with her dad, and I grab the couple of eggs the hens have laid since I checked them an hour and a half ago.

Then I stand in the doorway of the henhouse and peer up the driveway. Sure enough, there are two figures working on the fence. They're so far away I only know they're Carl and Jared because Carl lives here, and Betsy told me it was Jared with him.

As I watch, one stops and raises his arm in a wave.

I pretend it's Carl. I pretend it's Jared waving at his uncle's retreating truck. I pretend I don't care either way.

I scoot across the driveway and back into the house.

***

"So, what exactly is involved in a musical ride at a fair?" Betsy accelerates as we leave the village.

"I don't know, and I'm not going to find out. You know Lacey; she has these big ideas, but I'm not a coach, and I don't know anything about this class. She just makes it so hard to say no …"

Betsy laughs. "I take it you haven't met Bridget Sullivan yet?"

"No. I guess I saw her that evening at the fish fry, but only from a distance. I just remember a gaggle of giggling girls. Lots of people were talking *about* her, but I never met her."

"Well, let's just say, if you think Lacey's hard to say no to, wait till you meet Bridget."

"Which means what, exactly?"

"That's all I'm saying."

We pass Lacey's house, and turn down the next concession, and immediately into a driveway. There's an original wood farmhouse at the end – just like Betsy and Carl's, except without the addition they built on to make it possible to run the B&B – and, beyond that is a snug little stable block next to a paddock.

Three girls are leaning over the fence, holding out long strands of grass to two horses inside, and when we open the car doors all three turn to us.

"Meg!" Lacey runs over, her ponytail bobbing with each step. She's followed by a girl with tight curls, corkscrewing in every direction, that make me wonder how she fits a riding helmet on her head. "This is Carly," Lacey says, and my brain makes a quick connection: *Carly* = *curly*. I'll remember that.

The third girl follows them. All I see is eyes. Huge, almond-shaped, searing green eyes. They pop out of a narrow face, with a pointy little chin and scalloped ears.

Lacey said she has fuzz growing in, but maybe you had to see her completely bald to notice the difference. To me she's still a girl with no hair. I look, for a minute, at her bald head, then back at those eyes. "Hi. I'm Meg."

"I'm Bridget." She points at the grey horse, closest to the gate. "That's Diamond; my chemotherapy horse."

"Your chemotherapy horse?"

She shrugs. "Lots of people have therapy horses. I got mine because I had to have chemo. And he was the only thing that made me feel better during my treatments, so, he's my chemo horse."

"You ride a lot?"

"Now that I have him I do." Her eyes lock on mine. "Since I got better I make sure to do what makes me happy. Riding Diamond makes me happy."

She's Lacey's best friend, so she's around Lacey's age – thirteen or fourteen – but there's no wavering in her gaze; no hesitation in her voice. She's one of the most intense people I've met, of any age.

And I like her. I like that she said "since I got better," instead of "since I got sick." I like her because she's Lacey's best friend. And, probably, I like her a bit because of her story. For the same reason all those people gave away their money at the fish fry – what did they call her that day? Something like "Wonder Girl." Who doesn't like a wonder girl?

She tilts her head and smiles, and even though her face is thin, dimples appear. "Lacey figures you won't say no to me, so I'm asking – will you coach us for the musical ride?"

I glance at Betsy who's looking at me, with the corners of her mouth turning up. She told me so.

I take a deep breath. "Why don't you and Lacey and Carly, introduce me to those two ..." I point at the horses. "... and we'll talk about what, exactly, you have in mind."

Before I follow the girls, I turn back to Betsy. "Thanks for the warning. You were right. She's pretty hard to turn down."

"What can I say?" says Betsy. "I agree with them. I think you should say yes. You'll do a great job."

"Does that mean you'll be my assistant?" I say.

"It means I'll be the team baker."

"Yeah, well I bet these girls can go through a lot of cookies."

"I'm up for it, if you are."

"We'll see." I square my shoulders and walk toward the girls and their horses.

Chapter Nine

The main road on Ellicott Island is ridiculously rutted, even on a bike. Probably just as well I didn't bring my non-four-wheel-drive car over here.

I replay the instructions Adam gave me, "Second turn on your left. There's a big wood house by the water. That's us."

I bump and swerve down the road – second turn on my left – which turns out to be more of a driveway, since the only house on it is the big wooden one by the water.

I expected "wood" to mean farmhouse with peeling paint. What I find is sprawling seventies, probably split level inside, with patio doors everywhere. It's huge and, to my eyes, ugly. But the view is straight out to the water. Stunning.

"It's nine-oh-three." Adam appears around the corner lugging a sailbag.

"The ferry was on the island side when I got to the dock. I had to wait for it to come over and get me."

"OK, well let's go. It's going to be a great morning." He strides toward the dock, and I pick a tree to lean my bike on, and follow him.

"Is that what you're wearing?"

I look down at a plain t-shirt, jean shorts, running shoes. I have a bathing suit on underneath. "Guess so."

"Uh-huh. You might want to leave your shoes here. Without proper sailing shoes, bare feet are better."

I look at Adam's feet. They're long, narrow, and bare, and the uniform tan on them tells me they spend quite a bit of time exposed to the sun, so I guess proper sailing shoes are optional.

He wiggles his toes. "Are you checking out my feet?"

I straighten from undoing my laces and hope being bent over explains the red in my cheeks. "No. Not exactly. I mean, I was noticing your second toe."

"Ah, yes. Sign of intelligence, to have your second toe longer than your big one." He uses his foot to tap my own, now bare, very long second toe. "Or is it creativity? One thing I know for sure, people with longer second toes are always extremely physically attractive."

He's funny. Easy to talk to. Or, listen to. I've hardly said anything so far. And the physically attractive rule holds true for him. He's even cuter here, on the dock, with the river and the blue sky enhancing the colour of his eyes.

He holds a lifejacket out to me. "I have the boat ready, so we can just start sailing. If you want to learn how to rig it, I can show you another time."

Oh God it's tippy. I was on Cam's boat last summer, but I've forgotten how unstable little boats can be. It wows to one side, then the other as I clamber in, then Adam's feet hit the deck, steady it. "I thought you'd sailed before."

"I'm out of practice."

"Let's get you back in practice, then." I can't tell if he's flirting. Do I want him to be? Maybe. Why not? I'm allowed to flirt. He drops into the boat in front of me.

"Take this." He hands me a rope, threaded through a bunch of pulleys. It's attached to the thing I remember is called the boom. Because if you don't watch out, it'll bash you in the head. *Boom.* "And grab that." He points at what I recognize as the tiller. Then scootches forward and starts hauling on a line. For each downward pull he makes, the sail rises higher up the mast. At first it flaps in the breeze and then, suddenly, it's high enough to grab the wind, and the boom comes alive through the rope in my hand.

"Hey!"

He turns. "What?"

"What am I doing here?"

"Sailing."

"But I don't know …" I shut up. The sail's up and full. The channel's wide open and empty. And my body remembers. My brain can't explain why I'm cinching in the mainsheet, or pushing on the tiller, but my hands know it feels right. The boat responds. Jumps forward when I trim the sail; finds new momentum when I change direction by two or three degrees.

It's unbelievable how something so unlike riding can be just the same. How tiny movements make a huge difference. How you have to shut out everything else and focus. How the boat feels like a partner.

In a bold move, I pull the sail in as tight as I can, and the corresponding leap from the boat makes me laugh out loud. "Good girl!" I say, then remember Adam sitting up front.

He just nods, though. His white teeth flash as he calls, "Nice!" I think his trailing hand might even be caressing the boat's hull.

It would have been better if I hadn't started so well. I've fooled us both. "Ready to come about?" Adam asks, and I sing out a gleeful "Ready! Coming about!" and, at first it all comes naturally, but then at the crucial moment, when I think we should be turning faster than we are, and the boom isn't swinging over as quickly as I remember it should, I hesitate, and panic and start *thinking* instead of *feeling,* and I don't even know what I do with the tiller, but we're far too close to the water, and the waves are sloshing in, and we're going over, and we've capsized.

"Shit!" My life jacket pops me up. Adam's bobbing a little to my left. Neither of us is tangled in anything. We're not bleeding. The water's warm. It's OK.

I sneak a look sideways at Adam. I'm prepared to encounter a furrowed brow. Ready for him to ask what I thought I was doing.

Instead he laughs. Then lifts his hand out of the water; holds it up for a high-five. "Nice one Meg. That's your capsizing virginity lost."

Seriously? My capsizing virginity? But with his wet hair slicked off his face, showing a bright, white forehead against the rest of his tanned face, and with his grin stretching from ear-to-ear, I find I'm laughing too.

I give him his high five, then swim the few short strokes to the boat and, struggling against the slippery upturned hull, grab hold of the daggerboard. I pull it down, and me up, until I can step right onto it.

"Whoa! Look at Meg go!" Adam says.

The boat resists, then starts to go, faster and faster, until it settles back to the position it was built to be in; upright on the water. I'm not good enough to step straight in as it rights itself, but while I was settling the boat, Adam was getting into place, and he hauls himself in with one smooth motion, then reaches an arm for me so I can struggle and flop in like a landed fish.

We're turned into the wind, the sail's luffing – we're not going anywhere – so I take a minute to just lie on my back, dripping in the cockpit, and stare at the blue sky while I get my breath back.

"Where did you learn to do that?" says Adam.

I squint one eye closed, so I can focus on Adam with the other one. "I wasn't a capsizing virgin."

He grins. "Funny, pretty, and you know how to capsize. I'm impressed."

I roll over, shuffle inelegantly to my hands and knees. "Don't be impressed yet. I'm not positive I can figure out how to sail us back."

Pretty. The word dangles out there like an invitation. Like a worm on a hook. Like a carrot on a stick.

The thing is, I'm not sure if I'm hungry.

When order's restored, and the sheets are untangled and re-organized, and we're under sail on our way back to Adam's, I look sideways at the hunky sailor boy and think about that word again. *Pretty.*

It doesn't have to mean anything. I don't have to do anything about it. But it's nice. When my self-esteem's feeling particularly battered; when I'm lying in bed asking myself why my boyfriend chose somebody else over me, I can think of *pretty*, and let it make me happy.

The sailing lesson was probably worth it just for that.

By the time we get back to Adam's, just the seams of my clothes are still wet, and the part of my t-shirt covered by the lifejacket. Which is fine, because I can strip it off, and cycle home in my bathing suit and shorts.

I point to the boat, bobbing by the dock. "What do you want me to help with?"

He's crouched, tying the boat off. "It's OK. I've got it."

"OK, if you're sure." I hold out a ten and twenty, safe and dry in a Ziploc bag from my back pocket. "Here's my money for today."

He shakes his head. "No. We capsized."

"Uh, yeah. It's sailing. It kind of goes with the territory."

"I'm the instructor. I make the rules. If we capsize, you don't pay."

I hesitate. I'm still holding the money out. Adam closes his fingers around my wrist, and lowers it back to my side. "You can pay me next week."

"What if I capsize next week? What if I capsize every week?"

"Then you'll have to keep coming back, and that would be OK by me."

I leave him mopping the boat dry of the puddles left from our dunk.

On the ferry – piloting the ferry – a familiar face. Merry and white-haired and twinkly-eyed. "So, did you have a good lesson with my grandson?"

"He's your grandson?"

"My oldest, and the best sailor of the lot."

I push my hands deep in my pockets; encounter the damp there. "It was great. He did just fine. I'm coming back next week."

Chapter Ten

Riding the ferry, I delete five more I'm sorry messages. If I was still in a position to buy gifts for Jared, I might get him a thesaurus.

I cycle to Lacey's, where Jessie lifts my heart by thrusting her nose over the gate and whickering for me.

I lunge her, and she looks great right from the start. Her strides are long and fluid. "So, how about we jump?" Her ears prick forward, like she knows what I'm talking about. Jessie loves to jump.

Jessie loves to jump so much she's apt to leap a good foot higher than she needs to, and leave out strides, and run between jumps, and that's mostly where her unbalanced riders have been known to hit the ground hard, and fast.

I set up two jumps with ground lines on both sides, so we can take them from either direction, and I stride out the distance in between to make it a long four, or a short five.

I love this exercise when I'm schooling on my own, and I don't have anyone to change the jumps for me. The possibilities with just these two jumps are endless.

We start by jumping them one at a time; on a circle, from a broken line, toward and away from the barn. Jessie's breath comes fast and ragged, but I focus on what I need to do. Don't grab at her mouth, don't lean forward, wait for her to take off.

Whenever she gets really revved, I let the reins slide long, and rub her neck, and she comes out of her jumping zone and slows her stride, stretching her nose out.

Once we begin taking the jumps in combination, I start by asking her to put five strides between them. This requires her to collect her stride; keep it short and bouncy, so she can fit in the extra step between the jumps. It's not her strong suit, and we never get it done with room to spare, but we do get it done. It's a vast improvement from my early days riding her when we wouldn't have shortened enough, and I'd count to three, which would leave us, realistically, about a stride-and-a-half out, and instead of putting in two short hoppers, Jessie would just go; flinging herself – and me – over the second jump, leaving me struggling to keep my stirrups, with my helmet tipped forward over my eyes.

After several successful five-stride combinations on both reins, we move to doing the line in four. With most horses this would require some major lengthening. With Jessie it means I leave my hands light, and think *go*. I allow her to flow the way she wants to, and she does the line in four strides, leaving me with the impression she could have managed three.

Lacey shows up for the final test. We're going to do the line twice, without stopping in between. The first time I'll let Jessie go in four. The second time I'll ask her to shorten to five.

I talk to Lacey as I push Jess forward, framed up in a nice working trot; making sure she's listening to me before we begin.

"Watch this. She'll be motoring by the time we land after the second jump, and then we've got to canter around the whole ring, including down the long side where she'll really want to lengthen. Instead I've got to be collecting her the whole time. Guiding her energy up; not out. Making sure she's listening to me."

I squeeze my inside rein, and Jessie flexes into it. *Like this.* This is what I have to get her to do when her brain's already fried from jumping.

"If I don't have her collected going into that last corner, we're toast. There's no way we can get it done in the approach to the jump. You need to do all the work ahead of time, then just ride her steady."

Sure enough, when we land off the four-strider Jessie's ears are forward, every muscle is wound, and she's rolling.

Relax. I can't get her to, unless I do first. Then I jam my heels down, put steady leg pressure on her, and half halt. With some horses, this requires actually taking back on the reins; with Jessie, it's pressure – like squeezing a sponge – but she responds instantly. She comes back to me. "Good girl." I do it half-a-dozen more times down the long side, and going into the final corner she's balanced, listening, talking to me through the bit.

We round the final corner, her ears go to the jumps, she lifts over the first one, lands and *responds to my half halt.* This is the breakthrough we've been working on. This is what makes her rideable. I ask her for five strides, she agrees – it's a conversation; nobody's yelling – and when she lands off the second jump, I can let reins slide long, and rub my hand up and down her neck and tell her what a "Good, good girl" she is.

"Oh my gosh!" Lacey says with her eyes shining. "That was amazing. That was awesome. That's why you're going to be the best coach ever!"

***

An hour later, with Carly, Bridget, and Lacey circling me in the sand ring, I'm having serious doubts about this coaching.

Carly has already nearly collided with each of the other girls. Bridget sits tall and straight in the saddle, but I'm not convinced she's really doing anything. It's only Lacey – focused and hard-working – who actually has her horse engaged, but she's not used to riding with the others, either, and at least one of the near-crashes could have been headed off by her paying more attention.

Carly cuts Bridget off, Diamond's head flies up in the air, Bridget yells, "Hey!" Carly says, "Huh?" and I step forward. "That's it! Come on in and let's talk."

They dawdle in and stop facing different directions, then each rider twists in her saddle to face me.

"No! No, no, no, *no*. Who can tell me where the centre line is?"

Lacey brightens, points to the long line running from A to C the three of them are straddling in various places. In Carly's case, the muzzle of her chestnut gelding is the only part of him touching the line.

"Yes Lacey. Thank you. When I talk to you, you will line up on the centre line." Bridget picks up her reins and immediately begins clucking. "Not nose to tail along the centre line. Your horse will straddle the centre line, and you'll all face the gate, so that you're side by side and everybody can see and hear me."

Lacey moves Salem into place, then I stand beside her, and point to where I want Bridget's horse, and, finally, Carly's.

I back up. "There, that's better. Except I want to see you all sitting up straight. When you're on your horses – when you're in the ring – you're at attention. You're prepared. Show me that."

They all straighten their shoulders, which makes their horses shift and stand more square. "Much better."

"Now, I'd like to know a bit more about everyone's horse," I say.

"Even me? Even though you already know Salem?" Lacey asks.

"Yes, even you. In fact, you start. What's important to know about Salem?"

Lacey doesn't hesitate. "The main thing to know about Salem, is she can do anything. She can go Western, she can go English, she can jump, and she can barrel race. And she learns really quickly. That's why I think Salem will be a great musical ride horse."

"Thanks Lace. What about your horse, Bridget?"

The girl leans forward, and smooths a few stray strands of her gelding's grey and white streaked mane to the right. "Diamond's eighteen now, but the girl who rehomed him with me used to show him on the A Circuit. She even took him to the Royal. He's so talented and, even though I know I can't show him that way anymore, I want to do a great job with him on this ride, so people can see just a little bit of how amazing he really is." She pauses. "And, also he can do this ..."

Bridget gives her horse an aid I can't see, and Diamond puts his front leg forward and touches his nose to his knee.

I clap my hands. "Oh! That's amazing Bridget. That would be great for the musical ride. How about you, Carly?"

Carly's eyes are fixed somewhere outside the ring.

"Carly?" I repeat.

Lacey leans over with her crop and pokes Carly in the side. "Carls!" She turns to me. "We have to do that at school sometimes."

"Oh! Sorry! There was a butterfly ..."

Lacey growls. "Carly ..."

"Right! This is Shelby. We think he has some Quarter Horse in him, and some Belgian, too. He used to do farm work for my uncle and, before that, we don't know. He's slow, but he's reliable. And I love him. So, that's Shelby."

"I'm glad I know a bit about all your horses. Now I want you to walk on by riding forward until you reach the track, turning right, and walking with at least one horse length's distance between you and the horse in front."

I walk back to the fence, to where a woman about my mom's age is watching. She has thick, brown hair, flecked with grey, but it's her eyes that make the connection for me. "You must be Bridget's mom."

She nods. "Marcy. How long have you been teaching?"

I shake my head. "Oh, I don't. I'm not an instructor. Lacey has it in her head that I can do this for them but, you saw that ..." I point at the centre of the ring.

"Well, I did see a bunch of girls who didn't know what to do, and now I see a group of riders who look quite good."

The three of them are walking well-spaced-out, around the ring. All in the same direction. Nobody cutting anybody off. "It's better."

"It's a good start," she says.

A tiny start on an impossibly long journey. I don't say it out loud, though. She *is* one of their mothers. If she wants to believe this can work, who am I to dash her hopes?

Chapter Eleven

Betsy and I are working side by side, making pastry for the two pies she's baking for tonight's meeting of my Wednesday riders.

Betsy's living up to her promise to be the team baker, so I guess I have to live up to my half of the deal, and actually coach them. There's just so much ground to cover, though. Which is why the three of them are coming over tonight: Sunday.

"It's important not to handle it too much." Betsy uses a fork to draw pastry crumbs up from the bottom of the bowl and into the centre of the ball that's forming. "Baking's all about how ingredients mix. Warm hands will ruin pie pastry."

"OK." I copy her with my bowl of flour and shortening. "So, obviously I know Lacey, but what should I know about Carly and Bridget?"

"I have to admit, I don't know Carly, or her family very well. She goes to the village school with the other two, which is how they all know each other, and she lives further out than the other two – right at the head, and that's really all I can tell you."

"Well, I guess I'll get to know her."

"Now, Bridget is another story. Her grandfather took over captaining the ferry from my father, so I've known the family for a long time. And, of course, when Bridget got sick everyone jumped right into action ..."

I nod. "The fish fry."

Betsy pauses, lifts her fork in the air. "Of course, you were there, weren't you? I remember, at the line dancing after, watching you and Jared ..." She stops, shakes her head.

For a tiny minute the memory has me smiling. It was a beautiful night, late fall. Not really warm enough to be dancing on the lawn outside the community centre, but we still wanted to, because winter was coming, and it felt right to grab the chance while we still could. I stepped on Jared's feet, and he stepped on mine, and I laughed so hard my sides ached the next morning. "It was a good night," I tell Betsy. It's my turn to shake my head. "But about Bridget; I didn't hear much more after that."

"Well, she was in treatment a good chunk of the winter. You'd see her on the ferry going back and forth, and she was so pale, and, of course she lost all her hair ... but, still, she bounced back. She actually came back to school for the last couple of months, even though everyone thought she'd lose the year. People started calling her the Wonder Girl, and it's stuck."

Betsy peers in my bowl. "I think that's enough; now divide it and make it into two balls with as few touches as you can. Flatten them into discs, and we'll wrap them up, and put them in the fridge to chill. You can watch how I do it."

I eye two relatively equal hunks of pastry dough, and begin to shape them. "When you said I wouldn't be able to say no to Bridget, did you mean because she's been sick?"

Betsy pulls out some lengths of wax paper for us. "Well there's that, of course. It makes you want to do whatever you can for her. But there's something about her; don't you find? Something charming or, almost, bewitching?"

Those eyes.

Before I can answer, my phone gives a little chime, and vibrates in my back pocket. I freeze. My heart double-thumps. This is too much.

"Are you OK?" Betsy asks.

"I just ..." My breath's coming too fast. My hands are slippery with shortening. I elbow the faucet on and rinse them under the water. "I need ..." I take the towel Betsy's holding out to me. "Is Jared still working along the far fence line with Carl?"

I saw him there this morning. Saw his truck, that is, from the safe distance of the henhouse, but they could be done; he could be gone.

"I think so," she says.

"I'll be right back."

"But, Meg, what ..."

"Sorry, Betsy, there's something I've got to do. I won't be long."

As my foot hits the porch, I'm opening the message. Please let it be from Slate. Please let it be from my mom. Of course it isn't. **I'm sorry.** Maybe some people like those words, but I hate them. Every time I see them I feel angry, or sad, or a wrenching combination of the two. They've shone up from my screen at least two dozen times by now.

They won't anymore.

A quick glance tells me the truck's there – pulled into the field just off the road – right beside a collection of round bales. Perfect cover. I dive straight into the field, and the long grass comes up above my waist; slowing my steps, hiding ankle-turning rocks and rough spots. But I keep going.

Every now and then I look around for Carl and Jared and, finally, I see them about halfway along the fence line toward the water. I angle my course so there's a round bale between me and them.

Eventually I get to the final bale; the one right beside Jared's truck. I take one more look – I can't see them so I'm hoping they can't see me – then I dash to the passenger side, yank open the door, and shove my phone, with that infuriating I'm sorry message open on the screen, onto the driver's seat.

He can have the stupid thing. It's next-to-useless here, anyway, with the only messages that ever show up being Jared's endless, empty, apologies. I don't want them anymore, and I want him to know I don't want them anymore.

I shut the door and walk away without a backward glance. I don't care if they see me now.

When I step back through the door of the B&B, Betsy calls out. "Is everything OK, Meg?"

"Sure, fine. Do you mind if I just send a quick email to my mom and Slate? I need to tell them I lost my phone, then I'll get right back to work."

Chapter Twelve

B ridget's mom, Marcy, brings all three girls to the meeting. Lacey bounces into the kitchen, dragging Carly with her. She squeals at the sight of the two pies. "Can we have ice cream on the side, Meg?"

I laugh. "Sure, if you want it."

"Of course I do! I'll get it!" She puts her hand on the freezer door.

"Lacey!" I elbow her side.

"Oh, sorry Betsy. Is that OK? Can I get it?"

"Yes, Lacey. You may get the ice cream. I think there might even be two flavours in there."

I turn to Carly. "Would you like some, Carly?"

"Hmm? Whoops, I mean, pardon me?"

"Ice cream?"

"Oh, we're having ice cream?"

Lacey stands up and snaps her fingers in front of Carly. "Pie, Carly. We're having pie, and you can have ice cream with it, if you like."

"Oh! Yes please."

"How about you?" I look over Carly's curls to Bridget who's found a seat at the table, avoiding the pie-and-ice-cream flurry.

"Once the rush is over, I'll have some. Thanks."

The island school teaches several grades together so, while the three girls are in the same class, I know Bridget's younger than the other two. Looking at her sitting ramrod straight, waiting patiently for her dessert, you'd never guess it.

Once everyone has pie and / or ice cream, I clear my throat.

I have a blank pad of paper in front of me, a pen in my hand, and a huge case of imposter syndrome.

What am I doing here? I'm not a coach, and I'm not a choreographer, and I'm only a few years older than them, and this is never going to happen.

But Lacey, and Carly, and Bridget are waiting. And Marcy's waiting, and Betsy's waiting, although at least they're not sitting right at the table staring at me like the girls are.

I clear my throat again. "OK. I guess we have a few things to talk about."

"So, um, I'll say the things I want to say, and then you guys can say anything that's on your mind, and then, hopefully, we won't have to have any more formal meetings from now on."

Lacey reaches out, squeezes my arm. "Sounds good! Go for it!"

"First." I write a number one on my pad. Circle it. "First, is everybody needs to really pay attention to ring etiquette. We'll never be able to do moves where we come close to each other on purpose, if we don't know how to avoid running into each other by mistake. So, here's a print-out from the internet, of basic ring rules. It's stuff like pass left to left, and the rider working at a quicker pace gets the right of way – I want you all to read it, and memorize these rules, and follow them when we work together."

"Second." I still don't have anything written after number one, but it feels official to at least jot the numbers down. "I'm no choreography expert, but I think we need to base our routine off basic dressage moves. Circles, serpentines, changes of rein; stuff like that. We'll practice one move every week, so we have them down pat, and then putting them all together at the end will be easy. This means you'll have homework every week. If we work on circles together, you need to go home and work on circles during the week."

So far, so good. They're all nodding. "I also think it would be good to have one cool, unique, move we do. Something that makes the judges remember us. Bridget, maybe you can think about that. You have the trick horse, and you know what he can do better than I do."

"OK, the last thing I'm going to say, is we need one more person. The more I think about possibilities for the routine, the more I think three isn't enough. So, more homework; find us another rider. If anyone can think of somebody, let me know."

My throat's dry. I feel like I've been talking forever. I glance at Betsy, and she smiles and winks.

"Now, over to you guys. What do you want to get out of this? Lacey, let's start with you."

Lacey swallows a mouthful of cherry pie and straightens in her seat. "I just want to work with you, Meg, and keep learning more, and see what Salem can do, and have fun!"

"Carly?"

The sun coming in behind her auburn curls, makes her look like an angel. A dreamy angel. "Well, my mom says it would be good for me to have a goal. So, if I can work on something with my friends, that would be fun."

I smile. "Well, we'll try to keep it fun."

Before I can ask Bridget to talk, Betsy brings over a pitcher of fizzy lemonade and a bunch of glasses. She sets them in the middle of the table and squeezes my shoulder.

I'm grateful for the break, and I'm more grateful that we're almost done.

"So, Bridget?"

Bridget sits up very straight. She takes a deep breath and her eyes flash. "I want to move forward. I feel like I wasted so much time being sick. I want to get past that. To do things!"

"OK ..."

"No, really, I mean it. I'm *strong*. You shouldn't treat me any differently than anyone else. I can do everything they can do, or more." She looks to Lacey, then Carly. "No offense guys."

She claps her hand across her chest. "I want us to kick some musical ride ass."

The half of me that doesn't want to giggle at her serious tone, and her dramatic gestures, wants to jump up and start practicing right this minute.

Betsy's word was right – this girl's bewitching – or, at least, attention-getting.

"Thank you Bridget." I'm afraid I'll laugh if I smile when I say it, so I keep my face straight. "I didn't have any intention of treating you differently, but now that you've brought it up, maybe it's a good thing your mom's here."

I look over the girls' heads to her. "Is there anything we should be aware of with regards to Bridget's health?"

She shakes her head. "Absolutely not. She's doing great. Of course we pay attention to her health, and if there's ever a concern, we'll let you know, but for now, just go for it."

She steps to her daughter's side, rubs her scalp. "As soon as her hair grows in, there won't be any way of knowing she was ever sick."

Bridget squirms in her seat, and ducks away from her mom's hand. "Thanks Mom."

It's the first time she's actually acted like a thirteen-year-old girl. I don't think she'd like me thinking so, though.

They drive away, and I go back in to help Betsy tidy up the dishes. "You're putting a lot into this, Meg. I'm impressed."

"Yeah, well, it keeps my mind off other things, so I guess it's worth it."

And it's true; between my phone being gone, and the meeting tonight, I haven't thought of Jared once. Well, maybe *once*. But not as much as I normally do.

"Do you want a walk back down to the cottage?"

I normally say no when Betsy offers, but tonight I want to stay distracted. "Sure, that would be great. I can tell you some of the moves I'm thinking we can put into the musical ride routine, and you can tell me if I'm crazy."

"I don't know anything about it, Meg."

"Well, that makes two of us. Just smile, and nod, and it'll make me feel better."

Chapter Thirteen

W ednesday morning, instead of dying down as the morning wears on, the wind picks up.

By the time I hit the last hill before the Ellicott ferry turn-off I'm standing on my bike pedals, fighting for every inch up the incline and into the gale.

Even during the short, sheltered crossing, the little ferry bucks and rolls. I look over the whitecaps and my stomach knots.

I can't sail in this.

I'm not good enough; not strong enough. It would be like taking a beginner rider and asking her to jump Craig's powerful eventer, Apollo.

Insane.

Maybe I should just stay on the ferry and ride it back to the bigger island again; go straight to Lacey's to ride Jessie. But … that would be rude. Right? I should at least see Adam. Should at least tell him I'm too nervous to sail in this.

I tug at the hem of the brand-new, fitted, t-shirt I'm wearing. I'd hate to think I dug it out of my drawer, and snipped the tags off for nothing.

It's not like I'm in a rush – not like I have lots of other important things to do this morning. I'll go to Adam's, just so he knows I didn't bail, and see what he says.

An hour and a half later, with my feet under the hiking strap, and my weight cantilevered out over the scudding whitecaps, I can't believe I considered backing out.

If I hadn't come, I'd be missing this; Adam throwing the boat up against the wind, sending us flying along the channel. Racing my pulse, doubling my heartbeat, and splitting my face with a huge grin.

"I almost didn't come!"

He glances at me for a split second – "What?!?" – before turning his attention back to the boat, and the sheets, and keeping us from hurtling into the whipping water.

I watch him work – his arms and hands all long sinews under tanned skin and sun-blond hairs, his hair tousled in the wind, and the concentration on his face – and a shot of pure happiness runs through me.

Later, with the boat snugged against the dock, and the sails safely lowered out of the wind, I try to pay him again.

"Forget it."

"But we had a deal."

"For sailing lessons. That wasn't a lesson. I did all the sailing."

"You were *good*." I didn't mean for it to come out that way. For there to be that much emphasis on the "good." For my voice to drop on that word.

And I didn't think Adam would stop, and stare at me, and that when he swallowed I'd see his Adam's apple bob up, then down, in his throat.

And I didn't know I'd want to reach out my fingers and touch his neck, just there.

It's my turn to swallow hard. And then shake my head. *What are you thinking, Meg?*

"Um, can I use your bathroom before I go?"

He blinks, drops his gaze to my feet, then back to my eyes, this time with much less intensity. "Of course. Help yourself." He waves to the patio and the sliding doors leading off it.

I slide the door closed behind me, and stand for a minute, letting my pupils recalibrate from the bright sunlight outside, my ears adjust to the quiet of no wind, and my heart rate slow from maybe-almost-possibly feeling a spark of attraction to someone other than Jared.

I walk through a living room containing only a sectional couch, facing a massive TV. The view out the huge glass doors is completely neglected.

The kitchen is sparse and clean. A coffee maker sits on the counter. Nothing else.

In the hall leading to the bathroom are family pictures. Four people: mom, dad, a much-younger Adam, and an even-younger blonde-haired girl. Then a frame containing three of them. Now just Dad, with Adam maybe a couple of years younger than now; his sister about Lacey's age.

The bathroom – no surprise – is clean, basic: utilitarian. No candles or fancy soaps. No window covering. No decor at all.

The only hint of personality in the house is the second door on the left, as I head back from the bathroom. It's got a poster on it showing a girl riding a horse, with a saying scrawled across it, *A good rider can hear her horse speak to her. A great rider can hear her horse whisper.*

I step back out, and wheel my bike over to where Adam's hanging stuff up in the shed by the driveway.

"Do you have a sister?"

"What? Yes."

"Does she ride?"

"Why?"

"What's she doing at one o'clock this afternoon?"

***

"Whatcha' doin' Meg?"

"Pulling her mane." Jessie, bothered by other horses, driven crazy by all but the mildest of bits, and who skitters sideways away from a traditional curry comb, loves having her mane pulled. "It's weird how much she likes this."

Lacey giggles. "Can I do part of it? Salem just barely tolerates it."

She starts working on the opposite end from me and, with both of us combing and tugging at her neck, Jessie sighs and lets her ears splay and her lower lip droop. "No wonder you always keep her mane looking so good."

"So, have any of you found a fourth rider?"

Lacey shakes her head. "Everyone's at summer camp. Or visiting their grandparents. Or has a summer babysitting job. Or has just quit riding." She stops, puts her hands on her hips. "Do you get it, Meg? How can anyone ever quit riding?"

I laugh. "Well, it does happen." I look at her out of the corner of my eye. "I might have found someone."

"Really! I'm so excited! Who? Is she coming today? Is it a girl? Where did you meet her?"

"Do you know Alanna Turlington?"

"Oh."

It's so weird to see Lacey without energy or animation. It's worse than a normal person yelling, "No!"

"What is it Lace? Is there something wrong?"

She tilts her head to one side. "I guess not. I think she and her brother live with their mom in the winter – somewhere near Toronto – so they go to school there, and I don't really know them."

"Except ..." She giggles.

"Except, what?"

"Except Jared got into a fight with her brother once."

I drop my pulling comb on the concrete floor, and Jessie starts. I pat her neck. "What? Jared in a fight? What kind of fight? What happened?"

"It was a couple of years ago. At the family softball tournament. In fact ..." Her hands still on Jessie's mane, and she stares at the wall. "It was the last year Jared's dad was alive. Uncle Rob always organized our team. Nobody else likes softball ..."

I touch her shoulder. "You must miss him."

She nods. "Oh yeah. He had really big hands, and his callouses made them rock hard. He used to let me dance on his feet, and I liked it just because I wanted to hold his hands." She looks at her own palms. "I can still remember exactly what they felt like."

She blinks and looks right at me. "He was so nice, Meg. Like Jared in a lot of ways ..."

I bend to pick up the comb, and stay down a little longer than I need to. I want to find Jared, and hug him; help heal the loss of his dad. I want to find Jared and punch him, for ripping a hole in my own heart.

I straighten. None of this is going to get resolved today. The thought settles my mind a bit, but my heart is still churning.

Lacey exhales. "Anyway, speaking of Jared and Alanna's brother. It was a fist fight. Or, at least they swung punches at each other – nothing actually landed."

"Seriously? Why?"

"I think Adam was pitching, and Jared was at bat, and Adam hit him with the ball. So Jared yelled – just 'Hey!' or something like that – and Adam called him a hick, and Jared *lost* it and went after him." She shakes her head. "Thank goodness Jared had already dropped the bat."

"I can't believe it."

She shrugs. "Well, I think Adam had already said something earlier to one of Jared's friends about them all being rednecks. You're right, though, it's not like Jared, and it's not like the fight even turned into anything. My dad and Uncle Rob pulled them apart in about fifteen seconds."

"I've never seen that side of Jared."

"That's the only time I have. It takes a lot to get him to that point. I think something has to really hit him deep down."

I think of how he wouldn't leave the island after his dad's death. I guess Lacey's right; Jared can have extreme reactions, but they're few and far between. I guess I should be glad I got off with a slew of I'm sorry's.

I wonder how Jared would feel about me taking sailing lessons with Adam? I shake my head. He gave up the right to have any say in who I hang out with when he kissed Fiona-who-moved-to-Alberta.

I comb through the final bit of Jessie's mane. "Well, that's a crazy story, but it doesn't really have anything to do with Alanna."

"You're right. I'm glad you found her. I'm sure she'll be great. Who's she going to ride?"

I step back to eye up Jessie's mane. "Jess."

I say it firmly. Confidently. Like there's no room for doubt.

I haven't even met the girl, but I'm banking on her riding like the poster says; being willing to whisper to my sensitive mare. If she can, we'll be fine. If not, well, I can just add it to the long list of things I'm already not sure about.

***

The first three are out on the rail, warming up when a rusty Volkswagen creaks to the end of the driveway. Adam steps out.

"OK everyone. I expect you to do your own warm-up from now on, following the rules I printed out for you – in other words, not colliding with anybody else. I want you to spend at least five minutes doing walk-trot in both directions. Then we'll be ready to start."

A girl gets out of the Jetta's passenger seat. She's tall and bendy thin, with Adam's blond, blue-eyed colouring.

"Hi. You must be Alanna."

She nods. "Hi."

"So, how do you feel about joining us?"

She looks at the three girls in the ring – not running into each other, thank goodness – then at her brother, then back at me. "I haven't ridden for a long time. Could I watch today?"

We only have eight weeks. We don't have time for watching.

I bite my tongue.

We don't have anyone else.

"Of course. I was thinking you could ride my horse, Jessie. Maybe you could graze her, and get to know her while you watch today?"

So Alanna holds Jessie's lead rope, while the mare tears at the long grass growing around the edge of the sand ring, and Adam leans on the fence, and I copy Craig's lesson on circles, making the girls do ten, fifteen, and twenty-metre circles. Repeating things I've heard a million times. "That's not a circle; that's an egg, Carly," and "A circle has a centre, Bridget," and "If she's not bending, it's just a square Lacey – try again with more flexion."

"I'm going to put a cone in each corner, and you're going to ride a ten-metre circle every time you get to a cone."

I scuttle out to plonk the first one down, then turn back to do the rest, and find Adam's placed one, and Lacey's brother, Will, has appeared, and has already put the third one down, with the fourth one in his arms. "Thanks guys."

Will and Adam watch the rest of the lesson and, at the end, Will runs out to gather up the cones. "Leave them!" Lacey yells. "I'm going to have to practice. Right, Meg?"

"That's right. You all need to practice this during the week. Walk the ten-metre circles and work the bigger ones at a walk and trot. We want accuracy. We want bend. We're going to move on from here next week."

Will takes a pitchfork out, instead, and scoops up droppings from the sand. I wander over to where Lacey's running up Salem's stirrups. "What's up with the helpful act from your brother?"

She rolls her eyes. "Bridget."

"Ooohhh …"

"Yeah, even though she doesn't know he's alive." There's a tiny trace of something I've never heard before in Lacey's voice. Bitterness?

"You OK?"

She shrugs. "Yup. I've warned Will. It's not my problem if he doesn't listen to me."

Sure enough, Will detours by Diamond as often as he can, and it doesn't seem to bother him that Bridget never looks his way.

Instead she fixes her big eyes on me. "Thanks Meg. I'll work really hard this week."

"Sounds good." I watch while Bridget and Carly ride down the driveway, hacking back to their houses. Of the two, it's Carly who glances back every few steps, but that doesn't stop Will from leaning on his pitchfork and watching their back view.

Great. A complicated romance. Just what I'm trying to avoid by doing this. Oh well, I guess it's no big deal if it's somebody else's.

Alanna walks Jessie to me. "So, what do you think?" I ask.

She looks at Adam and he nods. "I'll try. But I feel like I'm behind right now. I'm afraid I'll hold you up."

"Well, I think you've made a good start by getting to know Jess. Why don't we meet up before next Wednesday and I can give you an extra lesson?"

Lacey comes over. "See, Alanna, it's fun. Are you going to join?"

"Hey Lace, why don't you show Alanna where Jessie and Salem get turned out. That way she'll be able to get her when she comes to ride."

"Oh, yay! I'm so happy you're going to do it. Come on. I'll show you the paddock, and her tack, and ..." Lacey leads Alanna away, and I figure Alanna won't have a chance to reconsider her decision with Lacey yammering in her ear.

I turn to Adam. "Thanks for bringing her."

He shrugs. "As if I could stop her. She loves horses. My mom used to take her riding. When she left, it tailed off."

"Can you bring her one day around dinner time for her extra lesson? Maybe Sunday?"

"Sure."

"Good. I'll meet you here then."

"Hey, Meg?" says Adam.

"Yeah?"

"I liked watching you. You were *good*."

My cheeks rush warm, and I put my hands to them. I know they're bright red. I pretend I'm scratching my nose.

I can almost picture the angel and the devil on my opposite shoulders.

Angel: *Be careful. This is the last thing you need.*

Devil: *It's nothing. It isn't for real. And it feels kind of nice. You deserve it.*

I go neutral. "Um ... thanks."

He nods. "See you Sunday."

With everyone gone I pick up a broom to help Lacey sweep the barn, and she promptly stops. "Man, I don't remember Alanna's brother being so super-cute!"

"You think he is?"

"Definitely, Meg."

"I hadn't really noticed, but maybe you're right."

Chapter Fourteen

How's the car? my mom asked in her last email.

Great! Love it! And I do, but I hardly use it. I still haven't had to refill the gas tank. I've been so used to getting around without a car, it feels like cheating to use it.

For days at a time it stays in its spot back by the lilacs and, sometimes I kind of forget it's there.

Whenever I think of driving somewhere, instead of biking, a little voice says, "Save it for a rainy day."

That's the voice that convinced me to take my bike into the village to get pizza for dinner tonight, even though it would definitely be easier to bring a pizza back in a car.

To be fair to the voice, though, it was beautiful at the cottage. Blue skies, with white, fluffy clouds, and sunshine flooding the fields. True, a glance toward Kingston showed a purplish tinge in the sky but, surely that was miles away – on the mainland – and wouldn't hit us till midnight, if ever.

Turns out, the weather was hovering in the bay just off the village.

I lean my bike against the railing outside, step into the pizza place and holding my helmet in my hand, running my hand through my flattened hair, I watch as the first fat drops hit the big, plate-glass window.

Great.

"Meg! Over here!"

Bridget and her mom are sitting in the corner, at a table for four. Bridget scoots over and pats the bench beside her. "Sit down!"

"We just got back from Kingston," she tells me. "I'm going to school there in the fall. We were checking it out."

"Oh yeah? I thought you had another year here."

She sticks out her tongue. "I could stay here for another year, but I want to *do* things. I want to work on my acting. I want to get on stage. If I stay on the island it would be my fourth year in the *same* classroom, with the *same* teacher. I wish I could go to school in Toronto, but Kingston will at least be better." While she talks her back is ramrod straight, and she uses her hands to illustrate the four years she's talking about, to point west to Toronto, then across the river to Kingston.

"Oh! Speaking of performing, I have some music ideas for the ride. We'll have to choose soon, right? We want it to be great." She nudges me, and I slide over so she can jump out from behind the table. "Can I have the keys, Mom? My iPod's in the car; I want Meg to hear these songs."

And she's gone, pulling her hood tight against the wind and the rain. "Whoa!"

Marcy nods. "I know."

"Is she always like that?"

"She is. She'll tell you it's because she was sick, and now she needs to make up for it, but I don't think that's true. She has a naturally intense personality."

Her eyes leave the window where Bridget just disappeared from sight, and swing back to me. "Speaking of which, can I ask you a favour?"

I started to learn about well-intentioned parental meddling questions while I was teaching horsemanship at Craig's. There was always at least one parent convinced their daughter was a sensitive snowflake, and needed extra time, help, and understanding. There was also usually one who believed their child needed toughening up. I'm trying to figure out which camp Marcy falls into, even as I nod, and say, "Of course you can ask."

"Could you keep an eye on her?"

I draw my eyebrows together, and purse my lips. "In what way, exactly?"

"Just watch for anything out of the ordinary. You can see she has so much energy. I'm worried about it being channeled in the wrong direction."

I take a deep breath. "I want to help, of course, but I hardly know Bridget. I'm not sure what I'd be looking for …"

Marcy leans forward. "Just anything that seems wrong. All I'm really looking for is another set of eyes on her." She sits back again. "It's a case of 'prepare for the worst, hope for the best.'"

We both turn to the door as a gust of damp air blows in. It's not Bridget, though. Adam and Alanna Turlington stamp in, pull down hoods, shake raindrops off their sleeves.

"Alanna!" I call.

The blond girl drops into the chair across from me. "I can't believe how fast it started raining!"

"You know Bridget's mom, right? Oh, and here comes Bridget. I haven't even ordered my pizza yet, so I'd better do that. I'll be right back."

I leave them all at the table, and go to lean on the counter next to where Adam's already waiting to order. "Seems like everyone had the same idea for dinner tonight."

"Yeah, my dad's teaching a night class at the university, so Alanna and I are on our own."

"Oh? Queen's?" I ask.

Adam nods.

"I'm going there." I say.

"Have fun. I'm not."

"No? Where …"

A girl wearing an apron comes to the counter carrying two huge pizza boxes. "Marcy?" she calls, then turns to us. "What can I getcha?"

Marcy taps Adam's shoulder. "I'm sorry to interrupt, but Bridget just asked if Alanna could come back with us for pizza." She points to the boxes. "We ordered way too much. Then, I could drive her home later, or she could stay over …" She raises her eyebrows. "Do you think that would be OK?"

"Uh …" we all look at Alanna.

"Do you want to Allie?" Adam asks.

She nods, her thin face serious. "Yes, please."

Adam turns back to Marcy. "That would be nice, if you really don't mind. She gets bored when my dad works late."

"We don't mind at all. I just wanted to tell you now, because I thought maybe you two would want to split a pizza instead of each getting your own." She elbows me, near my waist, where Adam can't see.

My cheeks flare so, when Adam asks, "Do you want to?" I say, "Sure. Yes. Anything but Hawaiian." Anything to send his attention away from my red face, and back to ordering pizza.

"You can thank me later," Marcy whispers in my ear.

And that's how I end up sitting at a table, across from Adam, eating what really is some of the best pizza in the world, answering his questions, and asking my own.

He's going to study journalism, in Halifax.

"Why Halifax?" I ask.

"Because it's not here."

"Seriously," I say.

"Seriously. I bet you like the island, right?"

I nod. "Love it."

"Yeah, well you didn't grow up here. And we don't even live on the main island. Do you know my dad gets cut off in the winter? The ferry stops running. It's a crazy way to live." He shifts in his seat. "I'm sure that's why my mom left."

"Left?"

He takes a bite of pizza, chews, and swallows. "She started teaching at Western half the year when Alanna and I were small, then, after that really wicked winter a couple of years ago, she got an apartment in London and now she lives there year round."

"So are your parents separated?"

"Not officially. I don't think it's my dad she wanted to get away from. I think it was this place. Which I totally get. And he's got three generations of living on Ellicott in his blood so he'll never leave ..." Adam shrugs.

"I heard you live with your mom in the school year."

He shakes his head. "Nope. We board at a private school."

"Boarding school? Really? I thought that was only in England."

He shrugs. "It's fine. It's not that far away. We can come back whenever we want." He pauses between slices of pizza. "But what about you? Ottawa's a great city. What makes you want to spend your time here on this hick island?"

Hick. The lick of anger in my gut isn't enough to make me slug him, but I can't just let it go. "I don't like that term."

"What? 'Hick?' Would you prefer hayseed? Redneck? Backwater?"

"How do you feel about snob? Prig? Self-important?"

He sits back. I wait. Is this where one of us swings for the other? A slow grin spreads across his face. "You're smart. Not a hick. That's very hot."

It's that word – "hot" – and that teasing, flirty smile when he says it, that make me realize this could be a date. I don't think I've ever had one before; a real date where you sit down with somebody else, and they're interested in learning about you, and you learn about them, too.

Jared and I just grew into being together. We sort of figured stuff out about one another, and anything we didn't know didn't seem important. We never did this.

"What are you thinking?" Adam's holding his pizza in mid-air, staring at me. "Have I lost you?"

"No. It was nothing, it ..."

"Meg?" We've been here so long, I've stopped noticing the door every time it opens. I look up to Jared's mom, standing by our table.

"Oh! Hi Mrs. Strickland." And then I'm not sure what to do. This woman cooked me Easter dinner. I've daydreamed about marrying her son. But I haven't seen her for weeks. *That doesn't matter.* I drop my pizza, and stand up, and open my arms, and she does the same, and we hug, tightly, and for a few seconds it feels nice and simple.

Then I drop back to my seat and realize this is more complicated than I thought. What would Betsy do? What would my mom tell me? *When all else fails, fall back on manners.* "Do you know Adam Turlington? Adam, this is Jane Strickland."

"Hello Adam. Your father and I sat on a committee together at Council." I love Jane's island way. Her polite consideration smoothing over any past awkwardness.

"Listen, Meg. I had to work late so I'm just grabbing dinner; I phoned ahead from the ferry." She touches my helmet, hanging on the back of my chair. "I saw your bike out there. It's pouring; can I offer you a ride home?"

"I ... uh ..." I look at her, then look at Adam. I live at the opposite end of the island from him. Driving me home is far out of his way. Maybe I should go with her.

"I'll make sure Meg gets home safely." Adam's boarding school manners mean the words come out firm, and sure, and gracious. Something flutters inside me when he says them. He nudges my foot under the table, and I nudge back.

I look at Jared's mom. "Thanks very much for the offer, but I guess I'm fine."

She nods, without smiling. "OK then. You take care."

And, after that, my stomach really is in a tizzy because I'm worried I've upset Jared's mom, and Jared is back in my mind, at the exact same moment that I've decided if Adam tries to kiss me when he drives me home, I'll kiss him back.

***

The headlights of Adam's rustbucket car slide over the shiny paintwork of my relatively new one. "Why were you cycling in a rainstorm when you have that sitting here?"

"It wasn't raining when I left."

"Or, you're stubborn." He takes hold of my arm, and squeezes it before I can protest.

That shuts me up, and my nerves keep me quiet, as he parks as close as he can to the porch, and we both dash out of the car, and up the stairs as fast as we can.

By the door, with the rain pattering on the tin roof, I'm having trouble thinking. How do I play this? Do I just say "thank you for the ride" and go in? Do I pause to give him a chance to kiss me? I've never had to plan a kiss before.

Adam saves me. "Is it OK if I kiss you?"

Oh, wow. That makes it simple.

He's so close, and, even though I'm tall, he's still much taller than me. I tilt my head back to look at him as I say, "Yes," and his lips are on mine. They're light, and soft. He kisses the middle of my lips, then each corner of my mouth, then moves back to the centre and, when I take a step forward, he takes hold of both my arms, and pulls me closer, then brushes his lips across mine, before stepping back.

My lips tingle, my stomach tingles, and my knees tingle.

"OK?" he asks.

"Mmmm. Nice."

Nice, but also enough, for now. I force a yawn. I'm not sure if it's believable, but it does the trick.

Adam smiles, and lands one more quick kiss on my neck. He whispers, "Good night," in my ear, and that sends a few more flutters through me. It's a perfect way to end the night; to go inside.

He watches as I step through the door and close it behind me.

He gives two quick taps on the glass, and waves, and then he's gone. Into the rain. Into the dark.

There's a delay while he lifts my bike out of the back of his car.

If it was Jared, I'd be out there beside him. Helping him.

But I'm happy to stay dry, and let Adam get wet doing it for me.

He starts his engine and I touch my lips while I watch his taillights recede into the night.

Chapter Fifteen

"**M**eg?"

I'm folding towels on the ironing board table, staring out the window to where a hummingbird's darting and vibrating around the feeder. "Yes?"

Smooth one side, make a fold, smooth that down ...

"Meg!" Betsy's hand lands on my shoulder.

This time I stop. "Yes?"

"You're folding dirty towels. Those ones need to go in the laundry."

"Oh. Sorry."

"Are you OK?"

I plonk the unwashed, but neatly folded towels back in the basket I pulled them from. "Tonight's Alanna's first lesson on Jessie. I guess I'm just hoping it'll go OK."

"Alanna Turlington?"

"Yep."

"Mmm-hmm."

I pick up the basket of clean towels and start folding the first one. "What does 'mmm-hmm' mean?"

"I saw Jane Strickland at book club."

"Oh."

"So. Adam."

"Yes. Adam."

"Well, what about Adam?"

I arrange the towel, square and even, on the edge of the ironing board, so I don't have to meet Betsy's eyes. "Adam is not Jared. And no, I don't know what that means, and, yes, that's all I'm going to say."

***

The truth is, I'm nail-bitingly, hair-twirlingly nervous. I should be nervous about putting a thirteen-year-old who hasn't ridden in over a year on a hyper-sensitive mare, but instead I'm scared to death of seeing her brother again.

What if he makes a big deal about it? What if he thinks we're all boyfriend-and-girlfriend now? What if he totally ignores me? Or, maybe her dad will bring her over instead. Would that be good, or bad?

When Jessie sees me she reaches her nose out, and blows warm air all over my neck, and I giggle, and breathe warm air back into her nostrils, and with our exchange all my butterflies fly away. It'll be is what it'll be. It's not life-or-death. It was just a silly little kiss. Quite a nice kiss, though ... *don't go there.*

Focus.

Adam's crappy car pulls up, and Alanna gets out with a smile, and Adam's smiling, too.

He says, "Hi." Then I say, "Hi."

Don't look at his lips. Don't blush. Be cool.

"Thanks for bringing her." I say.

"That's fine. What time should I pick her up?"

Alanna goes very still; turns wide eyes on him. "No, please stay. Just this time."

He looks at her. Looks at me. Shrugs. "Well, I guess I can. It's not like I have anywhere else to go on this hick island."

"You!" I swat at him.

He grabs my wrist. "Yes?"

His hand is strong. Warm. I look at him sideways. "Why would you say that?"

"Because you're pretty when you're angry. Alanna, isn't she pretty when …"

I pull my hand away. "OK, OK. Enough of that. Come on Alanna, let's go get Miss Jess."

I show the girl how to pull Jess's tail toward her, and knead the muscles across the mare's hip and croup. "She's always a little stiff, so this is good for her. Plus, she's the kind of horse you need to have a relationship with, and she likes this, so it'll make her like you."

I watch the slight girl for a minute, then step forward. "Here, see: really put your weight into it. She's not delicate. She'll grunt when you're doing it hard enough."

Alanna steps up and leans into the work. After a couple of minutes Jessie gives a deep groan. Adam, standing in the doorway, laughs. "Nice job, sis."

Now just for the riding part.

There are a million things I want to tell Alanna, but the gist of them all is not to take it too seriously; to stay relaxed and not to overthink things. Firing a volley of instructions at her will completely undermine that. So I have to figure out the best two or three, and trust the rest to the girl and the horse.

Before we take Jessie off her cross-ties, I walk Alanna to the door of the barn where we can look at the sand ring.

"You know your poster? The one on your door?"

She nods.

"Well, that's what made me think you could ride this horse. It's all about whispers with Jessie."

Alanna furrows her brow.

"If you get tense, or overreact, or yank on her mouth, that's like yelling, and she'll run if you yell."

"OK."

"We're not going to do anything hard, and we'll be in the ring with the gate closed the whole time. I just need you to listen to her, and I need you to listen to me. If I tell you to do something, I need you to do it, even if it seems hard. Is that OK? Are you ready to ride?"

"I guess."

"Let's go."

I hold Jessie while Alanna mounts, and the mare's stable manners are good enough that she stands quietly for me. I wait while Alanna settles into her stirrups, and arranges her reins, and then I walk beside them for the first circuit of the ring.

"How does she feel?"

"She's springy."

"Yup. That's Jessie. I want you to remember that's just how she feels; full of energy. It's not wrong; it shouldn't scare you. It's just *her.*"

"OK."

"Now, your reins are at a really nice length. I want you to leave them like that, and just keep riding the way you are, and I'm going into the centre of the ring."

As soon as I step away, Jessie speeds up, just like I knew she would.

Alanna tenses, just like I was afraid she would, and Jessie throws in a couple of jog steps.

"Alanna? Breathe ..."

She stares at me, while Jessie puts a super arch in her neck, and fiddles with the bit.

"Show me a big breath out."

Eyes wide and round, Alanna makes her mouth go round too, and instantly Jessie drops back to a walk.

"Good. Now push your hands forward an inch."

Alanna does, and Jessie stretches her nose, modifies the bow in her neck, and finds a sensible walk rhythm.

"Now rub her neck, just by her withers."

It's such a small thing, but it's the secret I found to riding Jessie. She loves praise. She's bold, quick, and long-striding, so you'd never guess how much reassurance this mare craves. Alanna pats her neck, and Jessie blows out through her nostrils, and drops her pace right back.

"Good. Nice. Now you actually have to squeeze her forward, don't you?"

Alanna nods, and puts her leg on, and the mare settles into a nice working walk.

"Done. You get this mare now. If you just stay this calm, and keep cool, you can do anything with her." I pause. "You're a star,

Alanna. There are lots of adults who would have her in a lathered frenzy by now. Great job."

The girl grins and, when I turn to face him, Adam tips an imaginary hat in my direction.

Later, after we've worked on the same theme through walk circles and up into trot, and Alanna's never panicked, and Jessie's never run away, I leave Alanna to untack and groom the mare while I watch from a distance.

Adam comes up beside me. "Nice work. Did you see me tip my hick cowboy hat to you?"

"You have a one-track mind when it comes to hicks."

"I do have a one-track mind about something. Come here."

I follow him around the side of the barn. He stops, and I run into him, and he turns around and cups my cheek with his hand, and gives me another one of his soft, slow kisses.

It's so nice. I'm glad he did it.

I'm also glad it's Sunday, and Lacey's in Kingston.

I want Adam to kiss me. I just don't want anybody else to see him do it.

I'm sure that'll change, though.

With time.

"Thanks," I whisper.

"See you Wednesday!" Alanna calls as she gets into the car.

Adam waits behind the driver's door while she settles in and does up her seat belt. "Yeah, see you Wednesday."

Oh yeah. Wednesday. Sailing. Alone with Adam who now kisses me. The butterflies in my stomach reawaken.

Chapter Sixteen

T he swaying, waving, wind-blown fields around the B&B are being hayed. The farmer who does them every year has started early, and is already mowing long lines in the grasses when I head up to work.

Every year I have a pang when the first grasses fall, and every year I get over it when the perfect, round bales start dotting the landscape.

At noon I carry my lunch to the deck washed in sun, and infused with the scent of fresh-cut hay.

I'm just finishing my sandwich, when Betsy pushes the screen door open. "Meg! Phone for you!"

Names flit through my mind. Lacey. *Jared.* My mom. *Jared.* Slate: no couldn't be Slate … *Jared.*

"Thanks Betsy." I put the receiver to my ear. "Hello? … Oh, hi Mom."

Betsy winks and steps back into the house.

"Meg!" My mom's voice is vibrant on the line. "I came home to let Chester out at lunch and there's a letter here from Queen's! Is it OK if I open it?"

"Sure. Go ahead."

The sound of tearing paper travels to me, and I picture the receiver lying on the kitchen counter, while my mom slides her thumb under the flap of the envelope. I imagine Chester panting by her feet.

"Oh, Meg!" The words are muffled, picked up from a distance, then they come fresh and strong to my ear. "Meg! They're offering you a scholarship!"

Queen's is my mom's alma mater. Queen's is the only university that didn't offer me a scholarship. Until now. My mom shrugged it off at the time, but this will make her very happy.

"You know what that means, right Mom?" I ask.

"What, Meg?"

"It means someone they already offered a scholarship to chose another school."

"Meg!" I'm glad my mom's in Ottawa, or she'd swat me. "It means you're being recognized for your academic achievement! It's amazing. I am so proud of you."

A lump rises in my throat. My mom doesn't throw words like "proud" around easily. "Thanks, Mom."

"You earned it, Meg. Now, how are you?"

I take a sip of Diet Coke. "Fine. You know, working, riding, coaching Lacey and the girls, sailing ... busy."

"Happy?" My mom's voice rises on the word. "I didn't hear happy in there."

"I ..." The easiest thing would be just to say 'Yes, I'm happy,' but somehow I can't tell an outright lie.

"Oh, Meg. Have you spoken to Jared?"

A chickadee lands on the edge of the deck and I flick a sandwich crumb its way. "Not *spoken*, no. He tried a few times. I ...

I asked him to stop." Suddenly, saying it to my mom, it sounds harsh. Maybe I was wrong. "I didn't feel ready to talk to him."

"Do you think you're ready now?" she asks.

"I'm not even sure if he wants to talk to me anymore. Like I say, I brushed him off."

"But *you*, Meg. What do you want?"

I'm not ready to tell my mom about Adam. He's cute, and he's fun, but our two kisses don't bring him into the realm of Jared and me. Of what we had. If Adam's still around in a month, I'll tell my mother about him. "I'm completely confused. I don't know what I want."

My mother takes the deepest breath I've ever heard. "I get that, Meg. I wish I could tell you what to do, but I can't. Nobody can. Even your brain can't. You might be surprised to hear me say this, but I think you need to follow your heart."

I picture my mom standing in our neat, tidy kitchen, with her back straight, hair shining, and clothes wrinkle-free despite the July humidity. I think of all those hours she spends in front of a keyboard, with a stack of documents, and a highlighter next to her. I picture the meticulous outlines she creates; all numbers and bullets, quotes and references. "Is that what you do, Mom? Go with your gut?"

Her voice is strong and firm. "Actually, yes. I let my heart tell me what I'm going to do, and then I use my head to do the best job I can."

Oh.

The tractor's up close to the house now; the engine growling in my ear.

"I should probably get back to work, but thanks for calling, Mom. And thanks for the advice; I'll think about it."

"Don't think too hard," she says. "That's the whole point."

***

When I go inside to replace the handset on the cradle, Betsy calls me from upstairs. "Meg!"

I walk to the bottom of the banister. "Yes?"

"Come up here, please!"

There's an unusual urgency in Betsy's voice. I hope I didn't miss cleaning a bathroom. I hope the toilet isn't overflowing.

I'm running through the list of possible disasters when I get to the top of the stairs.

"In here!" Sure enough, Betsy's in one of the ensuite bathrooms.

"What is it?" The stairs, and my apprehension, have me breathless.

"Look!" Betsy has both doors of the vanity open.

I hesitate. "I don't see anything."

"Exactly. What should be in here?"

"Oh! Toilet paper!"

"Mmm-hmm." Betsy walks out of the bathroom and leads the way into the neighbouring room's ensuite. "And look here." She flings both doors of the vanity wide.

No toilet paper.

Betsy is meticulous about supplies. We always joke we could keep going for several weeks after a nuclear strike on all the back-up toiletries Betsy has in the B&B. So, how has she run out of toilet paper like this? "What? How?"

Betsy hisses, "They stole it." She points to the next room.

"They what?" I picture the white-haired couple who stayed in that room. The only guests last night.

"They had a huge duffle bag. I should have known – I didn't see them bring it in, but when they carried it out it was full. I offered to help them take it to the car, but the husband said not to worry; it wasn't heavy." Betsy stamps her foot. "Well, toilet paper isn't heavy, is it?"

"Are you serious?" I'm fighting the urge to laugh, but I'm not sure how that would go over in the face of Betsy's anger. "They cleaned out *both* bathrooms?"

Betsy nods. "*And* the extra pack from the linen closet in the hall."

I shake my head. "But they drove a Jaguar."

"Well, they're not getting away with it. I'm going down to add a re-supply charge to their credit card, and you, Meg, are going to have to drive into the village and buy us some toilet paper since we have two new couples checking in this afternoon."

On the drive into the village I roll down all the windows, and let the wind tangle my hair, and sing out loud to the latest hit on Young Country FM. To distract myself from wishing Jared was here to sing along with me, I laugh out loud at people who drive a seventy-five thousand-dollar car and steal toilet paper.

Juggling multiple six packs of eco-three-ply I return to Betsy's car. Thank goodness it's a small car because the only parking spot I could find in the busy village was the last one before the river; under the branches of a low-hanging willow.

I pop the trunk open, and am dropping the toilet paper in, when I hear giggling, and smell cigarette smoke. I glance behind me, and would have looked away equally casually, and gotten in the car, and driven away, if the back of the girl's head I was looking at wasn't covered with peach fuzz.

No.

I grab a pack of toilet paper back out of the trunk, and purposely drop it on the road. "Whoops!" I say.

Two heads whirl around.

Bingo. Bridget.

What did her mom say? Look for "anything that seems wrong." This definitely doesn't seem right.

"Oh, hey Bridget." I stare at the cigarette in her hand, and then stare at the guy beside her. He's wearing the island uniform of jeans and a t-shirt. He has a bit of acne, but he's cute. He looks like he should be making himself useful, driving a tractor somewhere. I bite my tongue to keep myself from suggesting that.

"Hi …" Bridget whispers something to the guy, and they both scramble off the rock they're sitting on. He mumbles something that might be "See you later," before walking up to the main street, and she walks over to me. Still holding the cigarette.

I point at it and raise my eyebrows.

She drops it on the ground, steps on it, and sighs. "I know you're going to give me shit now."

I don't say anything. Just put the toilet paper back in the trunk and wait.

"I told you when I first met you. I want to do things. I want to *live*. I want to have *fun*."

God, how did I become the heavy at seventeen? Since when is it up to me to boss thirteen-year-old girls around?

Since I became their coach. Since this particular thirteen-year-old's mother recruited me as "another set of eyes."

"Bridget, that's the stupidest thing I've ever heard. People who want to live don't go out and start smoking, *which will kill you*, after they've just gone through a major battle to save their lives."

"Meg, I'm not, you know, *smoking*. I just did it this once, to see what it was like." Her big eyes widen. "I won't do it again. You won't tell my mom, will you?"

Should I? Shouldn't I? Whose trust is it more important to gain right now? Bridget's, or her mother's?

I close the trunk. Shake my head. "I'm not promising that, Bridget. For now I won't tell her. But if I think there's anything going on that could hurt you, I'll have to. I won't have any choice."

She bounces forward and gives me a hug. Suddenly she just looks like a young horseback rider again. "Don't worry. It'll be fine. I'll see you on Wednesday."

"Do you need a ride home?" I ask.

"No thanks. I've got one."

She turns to walk away.

"Bridget?"

"Yes?"

"You forgot something." I point to the butt on the ground.

She comes back to pick it up, twisting her face into a grimace. "That is so gross."

"My point exactly. Stay away from them from now on."

Chapter Seventeen

J ared's turning out of Lacey's driveway as I coast in.

He waits longer than he needs to before pulling onto the deserted highway. I slow more than I need to before making the turn. I look at him, and he looks at me. My wobbling handlebars break the wait. I shove my pedal down to regain my momentum and lift my hand – just a bit; to shoulder height – in his direction.

He nods, and lifts his fingers off the steering wheel. Then pulls away.

If I wasn't already out of breath from the long bike ride, encountering him would knock the wind out of me.

The pain's still there when I think of his familiar hands touching someone else's skin. His easy laugh prompted by someone else's joke.

But it's made worse because *my* skin's missing his familiar touch, and it's been a long time since someone laughed just the right way at one of *my* jokes.

I'm lonely. And I have lots of people around me. So, the truth is, I'm missing him. Missing the person I broke up with.

Thank goodness for Jessie. I don't think the world would need therapists if everyone had a horse.

Lacey's by the garage, squatting by a big green blob on the ground. There's a mechanical noise in the background. "What's that Lace?"

She lifts her face, and her eyebrows are drawn in. "I'm waiting to see. Jared brought it by. He hooked up the pump and told me to wait until it inflated. He says it's for Jessie."

"Oh!" I clap my hand to my breastbone. "I know what it is! Oh, oh, oh, Jess will be so happy!"

"Look." I point at the blob; rising, and taking shape. "It's an exercise ball. She had one at Craig's and she *loved* it. I can't *wait* to give it to her ..." I pause.

"What is it, Meg?"

"It's just ... it was really nice of him to bring it for her."

"He said he misses her."

I remember the look on his face the day I brought her here. Remember him saying: "I can't believe you just took her without saying anything."

I sigh. "I know he does, Lace."

"Meg?"

I brace myself for an open, honest, blunt Lacey question about Jared.

But Lacey's voice is less certain than I expect. Her tone less direct. "I kind of miss someone, too."

"Oh yeah? Tell me about it."

Her sigh is lost in the background noise of the pump, and the name she says nearly is, too. "Bridget."

Bridget. Two images do battle. Lacey's sweet, big-eyed friend, and the smoking, giggling girl in the village. "But I thought she was your best friend?"

"She is. I was so scared when she was sick. And I thought everything would be OK when she got better, but it's not the same."

The ball's almost done, so I switch the pump to low. "So, what exactly is wrong Lace?"

"I'm probably being silly. We just don't hang out as much as we used to. And, sometimes, I say something, and I catch this look on her face like she thinks it was the dumbest thing ever. And Will ..." she trails off.

"He likes her?" I prompt.

Lacey nods. "They're in the same grade at school and he's liked her forever. He visited her all winter, and I thought she was starting to like him too, but lately she's completely ignored him. You know, it's not as though she has to like him, but I think she's mean to him." She squints as she turns her head toward me, and the afternoon sun. "It makes me mad sometimes."

"I get it Lace, but I'm going to tell you something you might not know about Will, because he's your brother."

"What?"

"He's going to be amazing. I mean, he already has a great personality, but all you have to do is look at his skin – not one zit – and his hair –with that funky cowlick right over his left eye – and his feet – my God, Lace, his boots are huge; he's going to be about six-foot-two when he finishes growing ... your little brother is going to be *hot*."

Lacey wrinkles her nose. "Ewww ... Will?"

I laugh. "A minute ago you were worried about Bridget not liking him, and now I tell you he's going to have his pick of girls, and you say 'ewww?'"

"Do you mean it, Meg?"

"Lacey, both you and Will are going to have all the friends – and boyfriends, and girlfriends – you want. Bridget'll be lucky if you two have time for her."

Lacey twirls her hair, arches her eyebrows, and giggles. "I guess being completely amazing must run in the family."

Yes, it's true; I've still never met anyone who rocks my world the way her cousin does, and *no*, I am not having that discussion with Lacey right now.

I poke the ball. "This is just about ready. Let's put Jessie in the sand ring and give it to her."

The minute Jess spots Lacey rolling the big ball toward the ring, she freezes, head up, nostrils flaring, and ears pitched forward.

"Throw it in – it can even hit her – she won't care."

Lacey raises one eyebrow at me.

"Really. Just do it."

She heaves the ball over the fence, and it bounces once, twice, then hits Jessie's foreleg before bouncing off again.

Jessie explodes. She hops twice, then bucks, hind legs twisting high and, as soon as she's on all fours again, trots over to the ball, nosing it in front of her as she trots around the ring.

Every now and then it rolls to us, and Lacey, or I, kick it back to her, and that usually sets off a bucking frenzy again.

"Wow! She really does love it."

"It's good for her. We found she was sore less often when she played with it. I think it stretches out muscles she doesn't normally use." I snap my fingers. "Hey, want to bring Salem in, too?"

Salem isn't sure at first. She stands in the middle and watches Jessie circle around her with the ball. Then the ball rolls to me, and I kick it to Salem and, after one jump back, she reaches for it. She pokes it with her nose and, when it gives, paws at it. Then, all of a sudden, she drops her weight onto it. It rolls under her, and pops out the other side, where Jessie's waiting to run off with it.

Lacey and I giggle, and chase both horses, and Lacey kicks the ball, and it hits me full in the face, which makes us both laugh even harder.

"That was awesome!" Lacey says as we turn both horses back out in their paddock.

"Wasn't it?"

I lodge the ball in the corner of the tack room, and hop back on my bike, and I'm nearly halfway home before the first pang of loneliness hits again.

There are two ways home; straight along the highway, or cutting in on the gravel roads that will take me by Jared's. I wait so long to decide, that I have to make a huge exaggerated turn onto the side road.

Cycling up to his house sets off an ache in me. Salem's old paddock, that would have been Jessie's. The farmhouse that could use a coat of paint, but wouldn't look as homey with it. And the barn. The barn smelling just the way Jared's barn always has: of hay, shavings, cow, and faintly now, horse.

The chalkboard inside the door reads *Doc Farrow Weds* and nothing else. I find the chalk, lift my hand, and rest it against the board for a minute. *Don't be stupid – just write it.*

So I do. *Thank you so much. Jessie loved it. Meg.*

Then a wet nose nudges me. "Hey Rexie, boy." I ruffle the thick hair on his neck, and kiss his forehead. "I'd better go."

Because Rex is never far from Jared, and I'm not ready for more than a note, just yet.

Chapter Eighteen

I t's pouring when I wake up on Wednesday.

The pattering of raindrops on the tin roof pulls me out of sleep. The windows are just a blur of grey, with sheets of water washing over them.

So, what do I do now?

Surely Adam won't want to sail in this …

I know one thing for sure. It's a rainy day. *Thanks for the car, Mom.*

When I coast into the driveway, bumping over and into potholes, splashing little puddles out of them, Adam is under the carport attached to the house, with the hood of his Jetta propped open.

I park as close as I can, then dash under the sheltering roof. "This doesn't look good."

He drops his wrench, straightens, and a scowl stays on his face for a minute before he points at me. "*This* does. My morning just got a lot better. How'd you like a hug?" He holds out his arms, liberally smeared with grease. He's been in the rain; his hair is damp. He wears it all well: grease, frustration, and wet.

I step forward. "How about a peck on the cheek? If I can find a clean spot."

"It's not exactly what I had in mind, but we can take care of that later."

When I tiptoe to kiss his face, he wraps his arm around my waist – grease and all – and nudges his nose back by my ear; nibbles the lobe.

It tickles. I giggle. "You're filthy. Let me go. What's wrong, anyway?"

He steps back, and kicks the car tire. "Piece of junk. It won't start, and I know the part I need, because it's the same part I've needed the last three times it wouldn't start, but the garage in the village never has it, and it takes them three days to get it, even though there's a place in Kingston that always has about four sitting around. In fact, this time I'm going to buy two so I don't get stuck again."

"Well, take my car."

"What?"

"Take my car over to Kingston, and get the part you need, and do whatever other things you were going to do, which is probably why you needed your car in the first place."

"I can't ..."

"Of course you can. And you can do me a favour while you're there. There's a company over there that does t-shirts and jackets, and I called them about ordering some clothes for the girls to wear for the musical ride. They have samples we can borrow for sizing; you can pick them up for me if you go over."

"Really?"

"Really."

He grins. "You must like me to let me take your car."

I shrug. "Don't read too much into it. It's a car. You'll take care of it. You can drop Alanna and me off at Lacey's on your way into the village, and you can pick us up again whenever you get back. No biggie. I don't need the car in the meantime."

He lets down the Jetta's hood and clicks it shut. "Hmmm ... so in addition to saving my butt, did you come here to sail in this weather?"

If anything, the drops are pelting faster and harder. They're drumming a groove into the ground where they land off the carport roof. "Yeah, about that. Maybe not sailing."

"Not sailing sounds good to me. Come on."

The way he says "not sailing," makes my stomach flip, then flop. It's like "not sailing, but ..." The unspoken "but" has my nerves on edge.

"Come on where?" I ask.

"Inside, obviously. We're not going to stand out here all morning."

Adam's smart. Adam's funny. Adam is really quite hot. Kissing Adam has been nice so far. None of that means I'm ready to go into an empty house with Adam.

He pulls the screen door open. "Hey, Alanna, want waffles?"

Alanna. Of course. Stupid me. I breathe again, crowd in behind him. "Waffles?"

In stark contrast to her messy, greasy brother, Alanna appears wearing light tan breeches without a mark on them, and a polo shirt tucked in behind a belt. Her hair hangs in two neat, even braids down her back.

I know why Jessie likes her. Alanna's beyond calm – she's put together. This thirteen-year-old makes me feel supremely sloppy in my shorts and t-shirt with my legs wet from splashing rain, and my hair curling from the humidity.

Then she smiles, and there's a kidlike sparkle in her eyes as she asks her brother, "With whipped cream?"

Adam yanks his dirty shirt over his head, and I try not to notice the muscles sculpting his pale skin. "With whipped cream. I have to have a shower first. Why don't you get the ingredients out for me?" He turns to me, and I concentrate on keeping my gaze above his neck. "OK? I'll just be a few minutes."

"Yeah. Fine."

Alanna pulls out an index card, and starts meticulously arranging flour, eggs, and butter on the counter.

"Can I help?" I ask.

"Sure, you could get the orange juice and maple syrup out of the fridge."

I set them on the breakfast bar. "Your hair looks really nice. Did you do it yourself?"

She flicks the end of one of her braids. "Yeah. I always do."

"Is it hard?"

She stops for a minute, bites her lip before answering. "At first it was, but I'm used to it now. And we visit her pretty often."

My brain takes a few seconds to realize we're not talking about the braids. "Oh. That sounds great. In London?"

"Yeah. I like it there. And I like it at school. I used to be lonely here, but the chance to ride with you guys is fun." She points down at her breeches. "That's why I'm already dressed. Do you think we'll be able to ride this afternoon? I really love Jessie. I've been thinking about her ever since Sunday."

"You did a great job riding her. And, it's supposed to clear up around noon, so we should be able to get a ride in."

"What are we going to work on?"

I hand her measuring cups and spoons while I talk to her about the first bits of choreography I've been working on.

Adam comes in and, when he reaches over me to lift the waffle iron out of a high cupboard, he smells like baby shampoo and deodorant. It's the same deodorant Jared wears. It's probably the same deodorant half the men in Canada wear, but it's the first time I've really paid attention to it.

"Excuse me." I duck out of the kitchen, and down the hallway to the bathroom where the fan's still running from Adam's shower. I sit on the edge of the tub, prop my elbows on my knees and press my forehead onto the heels of my hands. *It's fine. Breathe. This is great. Alanna's sweet. Adam's fun. Breathe ...*

I don't cry. Which is good, because when I come out of the bathroom, Adam's heading down the hall. "You OK?"

"I think I got some flour in my eye. I'm fine."

"Do I need to help you with a closer examination?" He hooks his arm around my shoulder and pulls me in. He kisses my forehead, then my cheek.

I thread my arm around his waist. "No, I'm good. Come on; I want some of these famous waffles."

***

Not only does the rain dry up by noon, but the temperature spikes as the afternoon wears on. The wet horses and wet ground steam in the sun.

The girls have been practicing their circles. They're round and accurate.

"Perfect! You've all done your homework. So, here's what I think we can do with those circles ..."

I plunk a cone down and start to walk a ten-metre circle around. "You'll start your circle – your *round, perfect* circle – at a walk and then you'll start spiraling out."

Carly tilts her head to the side, and her hand flies up. I turn to her. "We'll work on spiraling out next." Her hand drops.

"When you get your circle out to fifteen metres, you'll move into a trot and keep spiraling out to a twenty-metre circle." I stop jogging through my demonstration circle and point at Bridget. "What kind of circle?"

"Round and perfect." I stare at her for a minute. She's just thirteen. She's experimenting. It's normal. I'm giving her the benefit of the doubt. *For now.*

"Thank you, Bridget. And then we'll reverse the move and spiral back in. Or we might start big, spiral small, and then go big again, and then all swap places. We'll figure out the details later, but that's the move we're going to try today."

I put them two at each end of the ring and get them to start on a twenty-metre circle. "OK, now start spiraling in."

"No Bridget, it's a spiral; not a nose dive."

"Lacey, it's not a circle if she's bent to the outside."

"Alanna, if anything, she needs to move forward a bit. Remind her this is work."

"Carly! Look where you're going. That was nearly a head-on collision."

Will appears from somewhere with pylons to separate the ring in two, and avoid future crashes. He places the last cone down. "Is this good?"

They're lined up perfectly in front of me. "Yup. Great. Thanks Will."

"Watch out!" I whirl around to see Bridget glaring at Lacey. "God, Lacey, pay attention."

Lacey puts her hand on her hip. "I was! We were supposed to start spiraling out again."

"Yeah, well not on top of me."

"You were too close ..."

Will clears his throat, and Bridget whips around to face him. "Oh just shut up, Will. We don't need your opinion."

Will's mouth drops open, and Lacey jumps in. "He didn't say anything! What is wrong with you?"

"Whoa!" I step to Salem's side and rub her neck. Reach out and stroke Diamond's muzzle. "I didn't see what happened before, but *this* is definitely not good ring etiquette."

"Whatever," Bridget mumbles.

I ignore it. "You're both fine. Riding in close quarters is part of the challenge of this kind of work. You need to help each other, instead of jumping down each other's throats. Now, go out and show me you know what you're doing."

Lacey picks up her reins. "Sorry, Bridget."

Bridget waits until Salem's headed back onto the circle before muttering, "You should be."

"Bridget!" I say.

She turns to me with arched eyebrows.

"I'm watching you, remember?"

She looks like she's going to say something else. I wait for her to say something else. But, after a minute, she just gathers her reins and heads out, too.

OK. Disaster averted.

My attention's caught by Bridget's mom stepping out of a mini-van and walking over to the ring.

"They're really concentrating."

I glance over, and at this moment, nobody's fighting, or running into anybody else. They're all spiraling in and out, with their horses more or less yielding off their legs – Shelby less, Salem more – they look like they know what they're doing. "They really are; and it's so hot."

"About that … I've got lots of space; what do you think about taking them all into the village for ice cream when they're done?"

She's right. It's hot, and they're working hard. This is all new for them. No wonder Bridget's a little snappy. No wonder they're getting on each other's nerves.

"I think ice cream is probably just what everyone needs."

I hope my doubts don't creep into my voice.

Marcy and I help hold the sweaty horses, while the girls sponge them off. "Let them graze while they cool off, and we'll talk about a couple of things," I say.

Each girl grabs her horse and they scatter – not too far – across the grassy area beside the driveway.

"OK, the things we have to talk about are a team name; we need one for the entry form. Music, which I think Bridget is already on top of. And money. This isn't going to be free, so is everyone going to ask their parents to pay for entries and trailering, and all the other expenses, or should we try to fundraise? If so, we need money-making ideas."

"And, I'm going to suggest we start this discussion in Bridget's mom's air-conditioned van, and continue it over ice cream in the village, if that's OK for everyone."

Carly puts her hand up, and I turn to her. "You and Bridget can turn Diamond and Shelby out in Lacey's sand ring with some hay, and you can come back here to ride them home after ice cream." Her hand goes down.

I sit in the passenger seat while the girls click through music in the back. I close my eyes, lean my head against the headrest, and enjoy the air-conditioned air wicking the stickiness away from my skin.

"Listen to this track," Bridget says.

"Why? Who decided you get to choose the music anyway?" Lacey asks.

"Because I'm the only one who knows anything about it."

It's bickering – that's all. Nothing heavy. Nothing serious. No need to intervene. This is supposed to be their project, and I don't want to butt in unless I have to. I'm just here to help them get it done.

And just like that it clicks. My goal. I didn't have one when we started, other than the final ride not being a disaster. Now I know what it is. I want these four girls to be happy. I want them to complete their ride and be satisfied with it, and then I'll be happy, too.

Marcy finds a prime parking spot at the Town Hall. If I'd found this spot yesterday, I would never have caught Bridget smoking. Part of me wishes I'd been able to park here; part of me is glad I didn't.

"You guys go ahead and get your ice cream. The ferry'll be here in a few minutes. I'm going to go down and see if Adam's on it. I don't want him to miss us, and drive all the way out to Lacey's," I say.

It's so, so hot. I should be trying to decide between a sugar cone or a regular cone; instead I'm baking on the unsheltered ferry dock, with the approaching boat still looking dishearteningly small in the distance.

I'm not the only one waiting.

"You look hot."

Jared's voice sends tingles racing through me.

"I'm assuming you mean I look hot in the sweaty sense, not in the sexy one," I say.

Then I wince. Using the word "sexy" in the first sentence I've said to my ex-boyfriend for ages is the polar opposite of cool. I hold up my hand. "Don't answer. Stupid question. I retract it."

He clears his throat. "I have this. I thought you might want it back."

My phone. Looking at it raises a lump in my throat. Those "sorry" messages he sent weren't that bad. I hold out my hand for it. "Thanks. I think maybe I overreacted. I'm sorry."

"No, it was probably me. But, just in case, I'm not going to say the s-o-r-r-y word."

The quiet we fall into isn't as bad as it could be. It's not icy; more awkward.

Until Jared breaks it. "Slate says 'hi.'" He nods toward my phone.

"I told her I lost it. She shouldn't have been texting me."

"I'm assuming you told her where you 'lost' it?"

"Why?"

"Because she likes to send messages every now and then telling me what an asshole I am."

"Oh." I try not to smile, but I can't help it. "What can I say? She's loyal."

Jared's eyebrows furrow. *Crap.* I liked us being polite to each other. Friendly, even.

"I didn't mean it like that. I mean, I didn't mean anything by it. I mean ..." I take a deep breath and meet his eyes, and they're still my favourite eyes in the world. "... I miss you."

The eyes widen. "I miss you, too."

By now the ferry ramp is down, and the cars are clank-clanking off it, and it's hard to hear, which is a bit of a relief, because I have no idea what to say next.

And then my name cuts through the clatter. "Meg! Over here!"

Oh. My car. I'm still not used to it. And Adam's got it pulled over where it's squeezing traffic. I look away from the car, back to Jared. "Thanks for the phone and, uh, that's my ride, so I'd better go."

The furrow's back in his eyebrows. "Sure. Go."

I slip the phone in my pocket, and drop into the passenger seat of the car. I guess Jared can text me now.

I glance back at him standing where I left him, and from the look on his face, I don't get the feeling he's going to.

Chapter Nineteen

I no longer have any such thing as spare time.

In addition to our regular riding sessions, working on serpentines, and riding on the quarter line, and the centre line, I've been having extra meetings with the girls to plan choreography. I draw moves out, and then we all walk them through in the sand ring before brainstorming whether they stay in the routine and, if so, where they fit.

Will's kept his distance since Bridget snapped at him, and I miss him popping in to hold a horse while one of the girls runs for the bathroom, or laying out rails to keep Shelby from drifting off the track, and just generally being helpful toting buckets of water, and sweeping the barn.

If Bridget misses Will, though, she doesn't show it. She's putting together our music, and spends a lot of time listening to tracks on her ear buds before playing them for the rest of us. More than once, when Lacey grabs Carly and does some silly dance moves in the sand ring, I catch that look on Bridget's face Lacey told me about. Like she's above all this. Like she's just barely tolerating Lacey.

I've been keeping my distance from Adam. Last week I asked Alanna to tell him I had to work, and couldn't sail on Wednesday – then I went and cleaned out the chicken coop for Betsy Wednesday morning to keep it from being a lie.

Alanna's gained confidence and independence, and often cycles to Lacey's by herself. The couple of times Adam's dropped her off, I've waited in the hayloft until he left, or made sure I stayed surrounded by girls and horses.

It's because I'm busy. That's what I tell myself. I like Adam; I just don't have time for a relationship. I can't be distracted. But, if that's true, why have I started running past Jared's again? Slowing when I go by his mailbox? Checking if his truck's parked in the driveway?

I'm too busy to even think about that, because, on top of everything else, we're fundraising.

It was Bridget's mom's idea. She's one of the organizers of the annual family softball tournament, which concludes in a dance, and she figured we could make tonnes of money by having a bake sale during both events.

Which means making sure we have a bake sale table, and signs to put on our table, and enough donations of baking to cover the table.

So, no spare time, and no romance. It's just easier that way.

I wake up and walk, yawning, into the cottage living room on the Wednesday morning before the bake sale to confront huge sheets of Bristol board covered with garish lettering and crude drawings of cookies, muffins, and donuts.

It's a good thing these girls can ride, because their art skills aren't going to get them far in life.

I tidy up the results of last night's sign-making party and, as I do, I think back to Adam picking Alanna and Lacey up last night and saying, "Sailing, tomorrow, right?"

With everyone waiting for my answer, I said, "Yeah, sure. See you then."

As the car hums along the highway, I think, *I don't have time for this.* As I ride the Ellicott ferry to Adam's, I think, *It was fun to sail, but I need to focus on this musical ride right now.* As I roll off the ferry, I think, *I don't know what to say to Adam.*

That's the kicker. That's the one that makes me squirm. I made him think I liked him. I do like him but … but ever since that day on the ferry dock, I've known the truth.

I wanted to stay with Jared that day. I wanted to tell Adam to just keep my car – drive away – I didn't care.

I like Adam, but I still love Jared.

Which makes seeing Adam pretty awkward.

As I drive along Adam's driveway, I rehearse what I'm going to say. "Sorry, but I can't sail this morning. Sorry, but I'm too busy. Sorry, it's my fault; not yours. *Sorry, sorry, sorry …*" It's a word I'm getting sick of this summer.

When I brake to a stop, Adam's there. He opens my door. He's holding a life jacket. "You came. I wasn't sure you would."

I take the life jacket but don't put it on. "Listen, Adam, I …"

He cuts me off. "Meg, don't say anything. Look at this day. There's nothing else anyone should be doing but going sailing today. Put your life jacket on."

The sun's shining in the sky, and dancing off the tiny waves whipped up by the wind. The billowy, white clouds serve to set off the deep blue of the sky.

"Come on, Meg. A friend of mine's driving out to Halifax next week and I'm sending the boat with him, so I can have it out there. This is our last chance – your last chance – to sail it."

I hesitate. It *is* a gorgeous day. I look at Adam. Maybe I've been making too much of this – avoiding him for no good reason. He's a nice guy, and a great sailor. And if this is my last chance to sail this summer ...

I struggle my arms through the life vest openings, and zip it up. "OK. But I can't stay out too long."

"Deal," he says. "You start."

So I take charge of the first part of the sail. Away from the dock – avoiding the shallow rocks which can catch the dagger board and hang us up – and out into the channel. Into that view I like so much; the points of the two islands framing the opening where the channel widens into the big lake. And onto the lake, the wind whipping us along, no problem at all. Today's wind is unusual for the islands; much cooler, and almost directly opposite to its normal direction, but near-perfect for this course. Which means getting home will involve a crazy amount of tacking, but by then I'll let Adam sail.

We sweep out from behind the shelter of Ellicott and I gasp. Partly at the expansive view of the west end of Kingston – of high limestone bluffs and imposing limestone buildings – and partly because of the dozens, and dozens, and *dozens* of matching sailboats all bobbing around in the lake.

Adam cups his mouth. "Cork!"

"What?"

"Canadian Olympic Regatta Kingston. The largest freshwater regatta in the world."

I can believe it. It's entrancing to see this many people sailing all on one stretch of water. It's also intimidating.

"Take over?" I ask, and he nods; we switch places. I'd be mortified if I got in the way of a race, or hit a support boat. This way, I can just enjoy.

With Adam pointing and explaining, I can make out the courses the boats are following.

"Out of my league!"

He doesn't deny it. I like him for it. I wasn't fishing for a compliment, anyway. It was just a statement of fact.

Back in the relative shelter of the bigger main island, Adam turns the boat into the wind, lets the sail luff, and we drift a bit. The waves slap-slap the hull, and I trail my hand in the water, and with the wind quieter, let the sun warm me.

"So ..." He shifts to face me, and his eyes are sparkling. "Make out?"

I laugh. "'Fraid not. Sail back."

The smile leaves his face. "Does this mean this thing – you and me – isn't going to happen?"

I suck my breath in, and he continues before I can say anything. "That sigh says it all. Why not? I thought we liked each other."

"We do," I say. "I mean, I do *like* you."

"And like isn't enough?"

"You said it yourself, Adam. You're going to Halifax soon. The summer's ending. We won't see each other anyway."

"Yeah, so, let's have an amazing fling. Let's go out on a high."

I shake my head. "I can't. I'm sorry. I just can't do it."

He looks at me for a minute. "I thought, for a while there, that we were on the same page."

"I guess I thought so, too," I say. "At first. But then I realized I can't just be casual about this." And then I say the word I spent the morning rehearsing. "I'm sorry."

I *am* sorry, but I'm relieved, too. I just hope it doesn't show.

Adam sails us back, and I'm glad the wind makes it too hard to talk.

He offers me his hand to step out of the boat, and it's warm and strong, like always. He pulls me against him, and I hug him, but when he wriggles his hands into the back pockets of my shorts, I push back. "It's still not going to happen," I say.

"It was worth a try."

I smile. "You get an 'A' for effort."

He grins. "Well, at least that's something."

Alanna comes to the dock as we're stowing the sails away.

"Hi Alanna. Do you want to come over to Lacey's with me?"

"That would be great. I'll get my stuff."

"Perfect. I'll say good-bye to your brother and meet you by the car."

We watch her run back to the house.

Adam turns to me. "Do me a favour and don't say good-bye. That way I can pretend you're just taking your time coming around to my charms."

"OK, how about I say thank you instead?"

He laughs. "That's more like it. Then I can say 'you're welcome.' My ego likes that better."

Chapter Twenty

"Change!" I'm walking out of Betsy's kitchen, balancing two perfect pies when it hits me.

"Pardon?" Betsy follows me to the driveway.

"I need change for when people buy stuff. And a money box, or something, to keep it in. Oh, Betsy, I can't believe I didn't think of this before. What else am I forgetting?"

I place the pies flat in the footwells of the car. "Chairs!"

"What?"

"We have a table, but nothing to sit on. Those shifts are going to be long ... I am the worst, most disorganized ..."

"Stop, Meg. You're fine. You've covered the big things. Carl and I are leaving soon. I'll rustle up a money box, and bring you a float, and Carl will bring a couple of chairs. You go ahead and set up."

It's a gift Betsy always knows how to give. The gift of calm. I'm sure she knows that what I need is ten quiet minutes in my little car and then I'll be fine.

I cheat and take more than ten. Halfway to the village my phone buzzes. It almost never does, now, since I told everyone I lost it. The only person who knows I have it back is Jared, so my heart beats faster as I pull to the side of the highway and check my text.

Have you fixed things with Meg, yet? Must be lonely being you. Jerk.

Oh God, Slate. Still telling Jared off. I thumb back a rapid response:

It's me! I have my phone back. You can stop abusing J.

Instead of driving off right away, I sit for a minute, and sure enough the phone goes again.

Does this mean you saw him? Did you forgive him? Are you back together?

The first and last questions are easy. It's the middle one that has me stumped. I stare out the window while I contemplate my answer.

Yes, saw. Together, no. Forgive? I don't know … maybe beginning to accept?

Her answer makes me laugh:

Deep stuff Miss Meg. We need to talk when it's not time for me to go to the pub. Which it is now – bye!

When I get to the fairgrounds behind the community centre, the place is buzzing. I drive past cars lining the residential streets all the way up, and every parking spot is taken.

Which is a problem, since I have about twenty kilograms of baking to unload, and a couple of tablecloths, and the big signs the girls made.

I step out of the car to contemplate my options when Lacey runs over. "Meg! Bridget's mom said you can bring your car right onto the grounds. There's a little spot by our table where you can park."

The girls unchain the gate for me, and I drive through, painfully slowly, trying to minimize the ups and downs for the pies and cakes, and cookies I have on board.

Lacey, Carly and Alanna are already at the table. We hardly get the first brownie unpacked before someone buys it. And it goes on like that; little kids tugging at their parents' t-shirts, "I'm hu-u-ungry, Mommy. C'n I have dat one?" Older people winking and paying twice the asking price for a cookie, "You keep up the good work, girls." And, thank goodness, lots of Betsy's friends who drop off baking contributions to keep our inventory up.

More than one person asks, "Is this the team young Bridget is on?"

Everyone's asking about the Wonder Girl. Everyone went to the fundraising dinner held for her last winter. All the churchgoers on the island prayed for her.

I suspect it's why we're getting so many customers and donations. People love that Bridget's bounced back and is riding. They want to see her succeed. Carly's suggestion for our team name was "Bridget's Dream," but the other girls, including Bridget outvoted her. The sign says they're the **WEDNESDAY WONDERS**. "We couldn't think of anything else," Lacey said. "And I like how strong it is," said Bridget. "And it's accurate," Alanna pointed out. "If everyone else likes it, it's good with me," Carly said.

It's probably just as well they're not called "Bridget's Dream." I ask Lacey, "Have you actually seen Bridget?"

She rolls her eyes.

"I'll take that as a no."

I mean to go look for Bridget, but I don't even have time to go to the bathroom. It's just so busy. We accept baking, and turn around and sell it within minutes. Everybody wants to buy raffle tickets to win one of Betsy's pies. And the girls keep running off to watch a friend's team play softball, or to buy a hot dog. I don't get to leave the table until Marcy shows up as it's getting dark, and the band's starting to play.

"Oh, my goodness! That's my part of the day done. Somebody else is responsible for the dance. Meg, you take a break. I'll stay here while you get some dinner and maybe have a dance or two."

"Are you sure?"

She taps the arm of the chair she's sitting in. "I'm not getting out of this for at least half an hour. I don't think I could even walk to my car right now."

"OK then. I'll be back soon," I say.

I'm three steps away when she calls, "Meg?"

"Yes? Do you want me to get you something?"

"No. Just wondering if you've seen Bridget lately?"

My stomach squirms. How long ago was I going to go find her? "Not lately. I'll keep my eyes open, though."

Marcy nods. "Fine. If you see her, send her over."

The man running the barbecue stand gives me a free hot dog, and I smother it with ketchup and mustard, and try not to think of my brother saying "Lips and assholes" every time he eats a hot dog. I enjoy every sodium-heavy, nitrate-laced bite.

The dance is taking place under the big cover that protects the skating rink in the winter, and I sit on the bleachers around the edge, and watch dads whirl their kids around, and husbands lead their wives out, and Lacey, Alanna, and Carly outnumbering Will.

Will stands still for a minute, and Carly bumps into him – her giggles float to me – I follow Will's eyes to see Bridget, leaning on one of the support pillars at the edge of the rink. She's not smoking this time, but the guy she's gazing up at is.

It's hard to say for sure, but I think he's the same one from the day I saw her in the village.

Lacey follows Will's gaze and shakes her head. She tugs at her brother's arm; pulls his focus back to their little group.

I sigh. I want to run over and shake Bridget. Tell her nobody but her thinks the smoking guy's cool. Tell her there's a perfectly amazing person just waiting for her. Warn her to think twice, be careful with the feelings of the people who love her. Not throw it all away for a bit of fun.

But that might be me projecting a little bit.

As I'm scanning the rest of the dance floor, my eyes freeze on a spot only about twenty feet away.

Jared. My heart seizes. My hand flies to the spot where my necklace used to sit. Still bare.

Just then he turns, and catches my gaze, and he stands stock still, too.

I'm a deer in headlights. Can't move. Can't think. Can't speak.

Wave. I wave.

He nods, and our eyes lock, and my stomach twists, and my thoughts scatter.

This is love.

This is all I've ever known, and I thought it was normal. But it's not – it's extraordinary – only one person makes me feel this way. And he's here, so close to me. Walking toward me …

"Meg," he says.

"Jared." My eyes flick from his high cheekbones, to his curling hair – for once not covered by a baseball cap – to the shadow under his jaw, before I realize I'm perched right on the edge of the bleachers, with no room for him to sit. "Sorry! Do you want to sit down?"

He clears his throat. "Um, I'm not sure."

Why is he so reserved? The knot in my stomach wrenches tighter.

"Well, I should get back to the table anyway … maybe you could walk with me?"

I hold my breath while I wait.

He nods. "Yes. OK. Let's go."

While we're walking, a yawn pushes through my body. It's caused more by my nerves than my tiredness, but he doesn't need to know that. "Sorry, nothing personal. It's just been a long day."

It seems to help. Jared looks at me. "You must be wiped. Do you need help packing up?"

Yes! "Sure. That would be great, if you don't mind."

"My pleasure."

Back at the table Marcy's started tidying things into piles. "Did you see Bridget?"

I hesitate. I decide I don't need to go into details; just push her mom in the right direction. "Um, yes. Over by the dance. At the edge of the pavilion."

"Great. I'm beat. I'm going to find her and head home."

I lift the hatch on the car for Jared who's holding an armload of Tupperware.

He drops it in. "So, this car. It's yours?"

"Yup. I got it after ..." *After we broke up.* Landmine. "Anyway, my mom gave it to me so I could get to Lacey's more easily to ride Jessie." *Because I moved her from your place.* Second landmine. They're everywhere.

Jared's smiling, though. "I'm glad it's yours. I thought it was... I noticed it at your place overnight a few times."

It takes me a minute, but my tired brain finally figures out what he's saying. "Please don't tell me you thought it was Adam's."

He shrugs. "Well, yeah. I did. I saw him driving it off the ferry that day."

"So, you thought he was staying over ... oh, no!" No wonder Jared didn't want to sit down with me at the bleachers. "Adam just took my car over to Kingston that day because his broke down. He was giving me sailing lessons this summer. And his sister's on the musical ride team."

Jared taps the window. "Well, it's a nice car. I like the colour." There's something almost bouncy to his voice.

It's tempting to leave it at that. To take Jared's relief and move forward. But lying – or at least hiding things – is what got us into trouble in the first place.

I lift my chin, and roll my shoulders back. "Jared, I should tell you something. I mean, I should be completely honest." My voice shakes. "There could have been something between me and Adam. There was – I don't know – the *beginning* of something."

Jared narrows his eyes.

"But, it wasn't right. I didn't want it. It didn't go anywhere, and it's not going to go anywhere."

I stand as straight as I can and wait. And wait. And wait.

He tilts his head to the side and exhales. "OK."

"OK?" *What does that mean? Ask him.* "What does that mean?"

"It means thanks for telling me. And also, that's not nearly as bad as what I was imagining before, so I guess it means, I can live with it."

My heart flutters. "You can?"

He nods. "People have lived with harder things. You have. I'm sorry, Meg."

I shake my head. "I'm feeling better now. I've been thinking about what's important."

"And?"

I hold my hand out in front of me. He places his palm against mine.

His skin is warm, and his touch sends tingles through me. I forgot what this was like. The longer I stare at him, the shorter my breath comes.

Then we both speak at once.

"Meg ..."

"Jared ..."

"Yes?"

I laugh. "You go."

He swallows. "Now that we're calmer – now that we've had some time to think – I was wondering if we could get together sometime and talk things over?"

I'm not the slightest bit tired anymore. "Yes. I'd like to." I lean forward, and whisper my next words "In fact ..."

He leans closer, too. "In fact, what?"

"In fact, I'd also like to ..."

"Meg! Meg! Meg!" Three voices ring through the air. Three high-pitched, giggly, excited voices.

I sigh and smile at Jared. "It's going to have to wait."

"What is?"

"You'll see." The kiss I'm imagining is perfect, and breathtaking, and it will be even better after I've anticipated it for a while.

Jared laughs. "Well, whatever it is, I'm looking forward to it." His face falls into more serious lines. "But I have to go to Simcoe tomorrow with my mom. We're moving my grandmother into a smaller unit in her building. Can I call you when we get back?"

"That would be good."

"A couple of days?"

"Great. I can't wait."

I don't even play the radio on my way home. Just let *I can't wait, I can't wait, I can't wait*, spool through my head on a repeating loop.

Chapter Twenty-One

L acey's buzzing about our bake sale profits. Her eyes are wide. "Six hundred dollars! I can't believe it!"

"Really?" Alanna just stares at her, then looks at me. "Is that right?"

I nod. "Crazy, isn't it? Now we really have to make sure we perform."

Alanna bites her lip. "That makes me so nervous."

"Don't be. I was joking. And being nervous won't do your riding any good." Jessie and Salem are tacked up, and I give each of the mares a rub on the neck. "Go ahead and take them into the sand ring and start your warm-up. We'll get going as soon as Carly and Bridget get here."

In five minutes, though, it's Carly alone who rides Shelby up the driveway. The big chestnut plants his face against me, and I straighten his forelock, while I look up at Carly. "No Bridget?"

She twists in her saddle. "I left her back there, talking to Will. I guess she'll catch up in a few minutes."

"That's fine. Go ahead in, and do your trot warm-up."

Bridget. I flashback to Bridget at the dance; avoiding the team; hurting Will. My stomach clenches. Then I think of the way the night ended; my moments with Jared. Much nicer ...

I shake my head. *Must focus.*

My plan today is to run through all the cross overs and cross throughs we have to get down pat to put the different pieces of the ride together. They're not technically difficult, but they'll be confusing until we drill through them over and over, and it becomes second nature for the girls to fall into their places.

We really need Bridget to be part of this.

The minutes tick away while the other girls progress through the stretching out phase of their warm-up, and move into taking up contact; starting some circles and serpentines.

Time to go find Bridget.

The dappled shade thrown by the trees speckles the driveway with sun. The wind's died right down, making it an unusually peaceful afternoon by island standards.

Except maybe not in Will and Bridget's world. The house blocks them from view, but Will's voice carries to me clearly.

"... whatever Bridget. It's your choice if that's who you want to hang out with ..."

She interrupts him. I can't make out all her words, but some drift to me. "Overreacting," and "Not a big deal."

Will responds. "Lacey was right. It's pretty obvious I'm your second choice, and I don't want to be anymore."

Now I'm close enough to hear everything Bridget says. "Lacey! How is this any of Lacey's business? Just because she doesn't have her own life ... Will? Wait! Will, come back!"

I kick some gravel. Cough. Call out, "Bridget? We're getting started … oh, hi there you are. Carly said you were just behind her."

Bridget's standing on the ground, holding Diamond's reins, watching Will's back disappear around the corner of the house.

Her shoulders go up, then back, and she turns to me with suspiciously glimmering eyes. "What do you want?"

Her tone's sharp, but I ignore it. Partly because I know what it feels like to be in relationship turmoil, and partly because I really, really need her to join in this session.

On the principal that riding always makes me feel better, I decide I'll let Bridget ride first, and see if it helps her work her troubles out of her system. I'll ask if she wants to talk after.

I leg Bridget up, and get her in the ring then clap my hands.

"OK everyone! Let's try this!"

To say we make mistakes is a serious understatement. We screw up many, many times. I have to keep referring to the sheets I printed off to double-check I'm sending them to the right positions in the ring. Even after the others know, more or less, where they're going, Carly can't get her head around it. She keeps drifting all the way to the rail when she's supposed to stay on the inside track.

After I hear "Carly!" for the sixth time, and look to see Salem's nose across Shelby's rump, I switch Lacey and Carly's positions.

"Now, let's try it from the top with everyone in their new spots. One, two, three, go!"

They walk forward four abreast and, at X, Alanna and Bridget turn right, while Lacey and Carly go left. So far, so good.

Back on the long sides, they split again, so that each rider will end up in their own corner. I look around to see each girl in her corresponding corner – unbelievable.

Now the crossover through the diagonal. There's a bit of hustling, and Alanna has to "whoa" Jessie, but no collisions, and everyone's where they're supposed to be for the last bit. This is where Carly's been having trouble. I hold my breath while they all walk out of different corners, toward the centre line, to set themselves up for the wheel.

If they do this right, it will be a total miracle.

They do it right. I can hardly believe it. "Whoo-hoo!" Lacey pumps her arm, and Salem jumps into a canter, and adds a little buck-hop.

I stand on the fence so they can all see me. "Good work! Excellent! Now we do it twice more. The first time showed us we're capable. The next time will prove it wasn't a fluke and, after the third time it'll start to come naturally."

I talk them through the next two run-throughs – reminding them of the moves, and where they need to be next, and also adding finesse:

"Lacey, she's not flexed enough."

"Carly, he really needs to step it up."

"Alanna, you're breaking your wrists again; no piano hands."

"Bridget, he's trotting around with his nose stuck out in front of him. He needs to engage. Remember: leg into hand."

I swear she sticks her tongue out, and there's no noticeable improvement in Diamond's action. "Bridget?"

"I heard you. I'm trying."

I'm not sure of that, but I remember her glitter of tears, and don't push too hard.

We make it through, and after, while the girls are clustered around the barn, and sponging sweat marks off their horses, and cleaning tack, and grooming, and chit-chatting, I wheel the barrow to the sand ring, to pick up the droppings from the ride.

I come back to a much-less-peaceful scene than I left. To Lacey and Bridget, squared off, with fists by their sides, and voices raised. To Alanna staring with wide eyes, and Carly's mouth opening in a gasp as Bridget raises her right hand, aims the hose she's been clutching square at Lacey, and pulls the nozzle trigger.

My brain freezes and I hold the handles of the wheel barrow for several seconds too long, until Will dashes past me, and I realize I can just drop the handles; I don't have to grip them, and so I do.

Will jumps between the two girls and yells, first "Aaahhh!" because there's nothing quite as cold as well water from a hose, then "Stop it!" I run up behind Bridget and grab her, but she just spins at me, and I get an icy blast before she aims back at Lacey and Will.

Lacey's yelling, "You're crazy!" Bridget's yelling, "I hate you!" I'm yelling, "Bridget!" when, finally, the water stops and everyone goes quiet.

Alanna's standing by the side of the barn with her hand on the tap. Smart girl.

It doesn't take Lacey long to start up again. "What did you think you were doing?"

Bridget's ribs expand under my arms, and I cut her off before she can draw enough breath to yell back. "No. Quiet. Everyone, take care of your horses. Bridget, walk with me."

She hesitates, but I yank at her sleeve, and she mutters, "Whatever," and comes.

Once we've walked halfway to the house – once we're out of earshot of the others – I stop, under a big tree and face Bridget.

She stares me straight in the eyes, and lifts one eyebrow. "Yes?"

"What's up?"

"Nothing, Meg. Everything's perfect."

"Come on Bridget. Obviously there's something bothering you ..."

"Or maybe there's something bothering you, Meg? Maybe that's it. Maybe that's why you give me such a hard time, and you're super easy on the others."

"What are you talking about, Bridget?"

"You know, I'm sorry if you're pissed that your boyfriend cheated on you with my sister. I can see how that would sting. But it would be nice if you didn't take it out on me."

The words in my brain make no sense, so the ones coming out of my mouth can't possibly either. "My ... what ... who ... your sister?"

"Fiona. My big sister. I'm sorry she went after your boyfriend, but it's not my fault." There's a twist to her smile that turns it into more of a smirk.

Holy crap. Holy, absolute, terrible, awful, hell.

Fiona. She said Fiona.

Oh my God. She said Fiona.

Chapter Twenty-Two

T he shock stays with me for a couple of kilometres. Which gets me over two of the worst hills on my ride without me even noticing the screaming of my leg muscles, or gasping of my lungs, that usually bring me to a pedal-standing, wobbling, near-halt by the crest.

I guess I fly right over them – I really can't remember.

By the third hill – just before the village – the rage has set in, and that powers me up and over the top with surprising ease.

I put my head down and pump through the village. *Please* don't let anybody see me, stop me, say hi.

If they do, I'll cry. If they do, they'll see me shaking; more than just from exertion.

I make it through, but just the thought of crying's brought tears. I can't see well enough to ride forward. Can't draw enough breath to fuel my muscles. I wobble into the ditch, leave my bike there, and climb up into a big field with a falling-down barn in the middle of it.

I trudge to the barn, past cattle who lift broad, patchy brown-and-white faces to stare at me, but don't scatter.

The abandoned barn is full of abandoned hay, which makes it perfect. I stand in the middle and think of Jared cheating on me.

Think of Jared lying to me. Think of it being someone from the island – of it being *Bridget's* sister. Wonder how much of an idiot I've been; coaching the sister of the girl who broke up my relationship. Imagine the tongues wagging.

All that speculation makes it easy to open my mouth and scream. I yell, and scream, and yell some more. The moldering hay absorbs it all, until my throat is sore, and my voice is hoarse.

And then I turn around, and walk back to my bike, and continue my ride into the wind, with no energy left to drive my legs.

It takes forever to get to Jared's. And I'm exhausted when I arrive. But my brain's still jumping around and, as I bang on the kitchen door, my heart's in my throat.

I peer through the window to the clock on the wall. It's after six. Where is he?

I have to talk to him. I can't eat, sleep – can hardly breathe – while I know this thing and I haven't confronted him.

I pace the circuit of the barn, the sheds, lay my hand on his tractor: stone cold.

Every now and then the anger starts to subside, but I stoke it again with an instant replay of Bridget's bombshell.

The sun's getting low, sending orangey rays slanting through the yard. Beautiful, but I can't enjoy them.

Finally there's an engine in the distance. The rumble of gravel under tires.

Jared's truck turns into the yard, and my heart hammers double-time again.

He opens the door and he's grinning: beaming. "Meg! I just got back on the six o'clock boat from Kingston. I was going to call you at work tomorrow to make plans." He jumps down. "I guess now I don't have to."

I clench my fists by my side. "No, you don't have to."

He lifts his chin. "What do you mean? What's wrong?"

"Fiona," I say. "Fiona Sullivan. Bridget's sister. *Bridget's sister!*" Trying to yell now, after my earlier screaming session, means my voice comes out raw, and cracked. It's a little scary, even to me.

"Oh, Meg." He steps toward me.

I put my hand up. "How could you? You let me think it was a total stranger. Even when you knew I was coaching her sister – her *sister*, Jared – you didn't own up to it."

"Meg ..."

"Shut up! This ..." I throw my arms out and spin. "This is the most special place I've ever been, and you brought what you did *home*, Jared."

"I didn't know, Meg. I didn't know it would be so important to you *who* it was. You asked, was it someone you knew, and I said no, because that was true – you didn't know her. And everything else was true, too. It was only once, and she's moved away, and I'll never see her again."

"But you *knew* her. You're both from here. It makes me sick."

"I didn't know her, Meg. I really didn't. I mean I know about their family – a bit – but she took French Immersion, so she went to school in Kingston right from grade one. Her family goes to the Catholic church, and we're United. That night, someone said something about me being from the island, and she heard and said she was, too, and I really didn't even recognize her."

"Bridget and Lacey are friends!"

"Yeah, Lacey's friends with *Bridget.* Not her sister. And I hardly even knew Bridget before she got sick and everyone started paying attention to her."

"We went to the fundraiser. You must have met her sister there."

"Why? You were with me. Did you meet her there?"

I'm not in the mood to let anything he says comfort me. This is proving me right. I was right to freeze Jared out all summer because *look what he's done now.* There's a perverse satisfaction in it. I look him straight in the eye. "Do you have any idea what it was like to have a thirteen-year-old girl tell me her sister cheated with you? And for me to stand there, staring at her with my mouth open?"

He looks at the sky, looks at the ground. "I'm so, so sorry. When I realized you were coaching Bridget … it was too late. I wished I'd said something before, but I thought we might get back together, and I didn't know how to tell you without screwing it up."

That gives me a new jolt of anger. "Well, it's really screwed up now. I was so excited about going out with you tomorrow night. I've been carrying that thought around all week. And now this …" I shake my head. "I hate this Jared. I hate it. I'm going home."

I grab my bike and wheel it down the gravel driveway. He follows me. "Meg, I was going to tell you tomorrow. You were so honest about Adam; I knew I had to tell you everything."

"Yeah, well, too late."

"Meg, please. I'll do anything."

"Leave me alone."

I hop on and start pedaling. He runs. "You can't go like this."

"I'm going."

I'm outpacing him now. He's struggling to stay near me. "Meg, I love you!"

I don't look back. Just yell, "I hate you!"

The minute the words are out of my mouth I know it's not quite true. I'll never hate Jared. But I hate what's happened today. That's true enough.

So I keep pedaling.

Back at the cottage, my anger threatens to drain away again. If it does though, what will replace it? Nothing good. Sadness, for sure. And maybe fear that my "I hate you!" did the job I'm not sure I wanted it to.

I pace the porch.

What should I do? Part of me says I should call my mom. She'd listen. She'd understand; she's known about this from the start. My mom would probably give me the same advice she gave me at the beginning of the summer – "This isn't the time to make decisions. Just sit tight."

Which is how I know she'd definitely tell me not to do the other thing I'm thinking of doing.

Because another part of me is remembering Lacey explaining how Jared lost it with Adam. Was so angry he swung a punch at him. And I'm also flashing back to Jared's relief when he figured out Adam hadn't been sleeping over at the cottage. When I told him nothing was going to happen between us.

If I was ever going to get back at Jared, Adam seems like the right guy to do it with. Plus he likes me. And he's cute.

I don't think I can sit tight. I need to feel better. I need to feel something.

I get in the car and drive.

***

My doubts mount as I ride the Ellicott ferry, but it's not like I can turn back. I'm going to end up over there whether I want to or not. I might as well drive the final few hundred metres to Adam's.

I crank the radio so the whole car's vibrating, and picture Bridget's smirk and, by the time I park, my pulse is racing again; adrenaline free-flowing.

I've never gone to the front door, and I'm not going to now. I head for the sliding glass doors and, inside, is Adam, leaning back on the couch, legs splayed, holding a controller pointed at a game on the TV.

I knock.

Nothing. He must have the volume cranked.

I could leave. He doesn't know I'm here.

Jared. Bridget's sister. Lies and deceit.

I knock again, hard, with the knuckles of both hands.

Adam's blond hair has fallen over his eyes, and he shakes it away as he looks at the door. He's wearing sweat pants, and a t-shirt with a hole in it. I have a mental image of the muscles under the thin cotton of the shirt. He looks like relief. He looks like revenge.

He yanks the door open.

"Meg? What are you doing here?"

I step forward, press my entire body against his, stretch up, and kiss him.

He drops the controller he was still holding, puts his hand on the small of my back, and pulls me inside while he kisses me back.

With his other hand he slides the door shut. The night disappears, and now there's just our reflection in the glass. Two bodies pressed together. My hands sliding under his shirt. His reaching for my backside.

I get the shirt up, and run my hands over his tight skin. His muscles. His ribs. I kiss his chest.

"God, Meg. Where'd all that resistance go?"

I move my lips to his neck. "Is Alanna here?"

"Sleeping over with Lacey." *Nice.*

"Your dad?"

"Working late."

"Good."

"Good? Who are you? What happened?"

"Shut up." I use my lips to shut him up, and he responds. We kiss and kiss, until my lips are sore. Until the stubble on his cheeks roughens the skin on mine.

He pulls me to the couch, flicking off the lamp at the end that makes this room a fishbowl to anyone looking in from outside. He lies down, and pulls me beside him, and the couch is old and soft, so I roll tight to his body and it's warm, and nice, and comforting.

But that's not why I'm here. That's not what Adam's for.

I take his hand and place it on my breast and he groans, but I feel nothing. I feel a hand on my breast, but that's it. Nothing deeper. No tingling, no shocks. No pull deep inside me.

Shit.

Now he's found the hem of my shirt, and he's pushing it up, and his hand trails across my bare skin … and it's just a hand.

"Oh God Meg. I've been waiting for this."

"Mmmm …"

"You are so beautiful."

"Mmmm …"

He kisses me while his hand rests on my bra cup, and I kiss him back, but it's all teeth, and tongues, and lips, and trying to figure out where they should go.

He stops. Meets my eyes. "You're not into this anymore, are you?"

"I …" Oh great. Now on top of jealous, and angry, and stupid, I feel guilty. And a bit dirty. The waistband of my pants has pushed down, and I grab it and wriggle it back into place. "We could keep, you know, kissing."

"Yeah, thanks. That sounds like fun. Kissing a girl who doesn't want to be kissing me."

"It's not that I don't want to. I actually really, really want to …"

"But?"

Don't talk about Jared. Don't think about Jared. Don't be that girl.

The only thing I can think of that would be worse than leading Adam on, would be leading him on, only to then talk about my ex-boyfriend.

"But, I'm a bit screwed up."

"You think I don't know that? You think my sister hasn't heard every detail from his cousin, and told me everything? But so what? This isn't that. I'm going to Halifax in a few weeks. You're starting university. I like you. You're gorgeous." He sighs. "I think this could have been so much fun. I wish it could have."

I press my face against his breastbone, and my voice comes out muffled. "I sort of wish it could have too."

"'Sort of.' Ringing endorsement there."

"Could we just count this as an affectionate good-bye?" I pull back so I can look him in the eye.

"Affection wasn't really what I was after." His voice is growly, but he puts his arm around me, and I'm so relieved that he's not shoving me off the couch, and marching me out the door. And it's warm, and his skin is soft, and the rise and fall of his chest is rhythmic, and I'm so, so tired …

… Water running. Or something. A noise in the house. I blink out of the darkness behind my eyelids to the washy light thrown by the still-on TV.

Adam's next to me, eyes closed, mouth parted, breathing deeply but not-quite-snoring. Chest bare. My whole left side is stiff from being pushed into the sofa. My shirt's rucked up, but still on.

The rush of water stops. A toilet finishing the flush cycle. Which means Adam's dad is home. Which means he saw me – us – sprawled on the couch, clothes twisted. Adam shirtless.

Classy, Meg.

I have to go. I want to be home now. Wish I'd never come. Why did I come? Why didn't I call my mom, then go up to Betsy and Carl's, and ask to watch a British mystery show on PBS with them, while eating a pint of ice cream?

I bite my lip; feel for the floor with my right foot and right hand. Once both touch the carpet, I transfer my weight onto them.

Adam snorts and mutters.

I freeze and count to thirty. Slowly. I can't wake him up. I can't face anyone right now. I need to be alone, in my bed.

Which is where I'd be if I'd gone to Betsy and Carl's. Instead I'm trying to sneak out of a guy's house without waking him up.

Nice move.

With Adam settled again, I take a deep breath, then roll, in one fast, smooth motion, onto the floor.

I hold my breath and wait. No sound. No springs creaking. Nothing.

I crawl across the floor, crack the door, slip through, and I'm out in the dark, and there's relief in being exposed to the dropping temperature and the building wind.

My car starts quietly. *Good little car.*

I wince at the green numbers of the dashboard clock. One-twenty. *Crap.* I don't even know if the ferry's still running. What am I going to do if I'm stuck here until morning? I really don't want Jared to know about this. The thought of him finding out sends a dagger of panic through me. The longer I stay here, the more chance he'll find out.

"Whoa!" My voice, breaking the silence, calms me. "First see if the ferry's running. Then freak out."

I pull up to the empty ferry dock. Now what? I flash my headlights twice, then turn off the engine to wait.

The cold seeps in quickly. Turns out it's cold in August at one-thirty in the morning. I shiver and wrap my arms around myself.

Well, I really screwed this up.

I wince to think of Adam's opinion of me. And his dad must assume I'm a complete skank. And Jared ... I shudder. Oh my God. If Jared finds out I came straight to the guy he hates most in the world ... my brain blanks out on that thought.

All this time, all this summer, I've been up on my high-horse. The wronged one. The victim. In the back of my mind, I've thought

I could get back together with Jared if I just decided to. Now, I'm the one who's done something wrong. I thought I deserved revenge. I thought it would feel great. And it doesn't matter that I pulled out at the last minute, because it's getting closer and closer to two a.m. and *this looks so bad*.

OK, calm down. It could be worse. I could have ignored my better judgment and kept going with Adam; then I'd really have something to regret. I could have been naked on the couch when his dad came home. The ferry might not have come ...

The ferry!

Things are looking up.

I ease the car into the dead centre of the tiny boat, put on the parking brake, and roll down the window when the captain – someone I've never seen before – comes to the side of the car. Thank God Adam's grandfather doesn't work the late night shift.

"I was afraid you wouldn't be running anymore."

"I shouldn't be – you got lucky – I happened to see your lights and thought 'what the heck?'"

"Well, thanks. You're a lifesaver."

"My pleasure. You get home safe now."

I get home safe on empty roads. I don't even see a deer. When I turn onto the cottage road, the beams of my headlights sweep across a herd of cows. Their eyes pinpoint, then fade away.

It's my inner thoughts that are dangerous. The twisting stew of guilt, regret and anger at myself. I should have known better. I *did* know better. I was petty. I was pathetic. I'm embarrassed. I'm ashamed.

I'm also exhausted. Yawning so wide my jaw cracks. I hope that means I'll be able to sleep. Then I'll wake up and it'll be a fresh day, and I'll run, and go to work, and try to forget about all this happening.

Oh.

Jared's truck is at the end of my driveway.

No.

I park behind him. I don't know why I bother being quiet; my brights slicing through the thick island night have already announced my arrival.

I step out of my flip-flops and pad up the stairs, missing the creaky bits in the middle, holding my breath, not knowing what to expect.

He's asleep on the porch in front of the door. I'd have to step over him to get in.

I walk right up to him, and look down. His sweatshirt is balled under his head, baseball cap skewed to the side, arms crossed over his chest, legs relaxed, feet turned out.

He's not as tall as Adam, or as blond. He's not the guy you'd notice the minute he walked into a crowded room. Unless you were me. He's the guy I'd notice in any room, any time. Or unless he smiled. That smile like the sun coming out. I miss it.

As badly as I wanted to roll and creep away from Adam earlier, I want to lie down next to Jared now.

I shift, and my movement triggers the motion sensor in the porch light. Jared stretches and blinks. "Meg." He smiles, then he blinks again, and stops smiling.

He scrambles up fast, too fast for me to do anything but watch him. "Sailing lessons run a little late?" There's nothing light in his voice.

Adrenaline floods me; racing my heart, speeding my words. "It's not like that. It's not what you think."

He looks at his wrist. "I think it's two-oh-seven a.m., Meg."

"I know. It looks bad. Yes, I went to Adam's. Yes, I wanted to get back at you."

There's a tic at Jared's temple, and his nostrils flare.

"I know, it's stupid, but I was angry. And my feelings were hurt." I hold onto his eye contact. I hope he'll listen if I can just keep him looking at me. "But I couldn't go through with it. Everything about it was wrong. We said good-bye."

"So then you stayed until the middle of the night 'saying good-bye?'" I hardly recognize Jared's voice laden with sarcasm.

"So then I fell asleep on the couch, in the living room."

"Why should I believe you?"

I stand up straighter. "Because I told you the truth before."

I know Jared's considering my words, because he looks away from me, then back. Because he tightens his lips together in a straight line.

He shakes his head. "I don't know, Meg. I hurt you; you hurt me. Maybe I started a cycle we can't break out of." He takes a step away from me. "Maybe this has gone too far to rescue."

"Jared. Wait …"

"Wait for what? I think I've waited long enough tonight."

"Stop!" He halts. Half faces me. I've found some of my anger again. "That's it? That's all you've got? We've come to this point – to this terrible point – to what might be the end, and you're just going to walk away?"

"What do you want from me, Meg?"

"I want something more. I want you to care. Lacey told me you hit Adam when he got in your face. You wouldn't leave this island for nearly a year after your dad died. But we end, and you just do ... what? I don't even know. Call me crazy but I guess I want a grand gesture. An indication you care."

Jared takes two steps toward me. Two heavy, loud steps. He grips the railing, and he's shaking. "Don't you even, Meg ... You threw my messages back in my face. You told me to leave you alone. You told me you hate me. And then I come and lie on this hard porch, and cramp up from the cold, and spend half my time imagining you dead in a ditch, and the other half imagining you with *him*, and you want a gesture from me?"

He throws up his hands. "This is what I've got. This was my gesture. If it's not good enough for you, then I guess I'm not either."

I open my mouth but I can't make words come out against the air I'm sucking in.

I'm sorry.

You're right.

I didn't see it until now.

I need you.

They all stay in my head.

And, in the meantime, Jared's engine's started. He's rolling onto the gravel of the driveway. He's driving away.

He's driving away.

Chapter Twenty-Three

I don't fall asleep until the sun comes up. *Just a little nap*, I think, and then don't wake up until Betsy comes knocking on the door.

Twice in twelve hours sleeping when I shouldn't has got me in trouble.

Betsy draws her eyebrows together when she sees me. "Are you sick?"

"No."

Yes.

I'm sick in the pit of my stomach. I'm heartsick. I'm sick of life without Jared. Which I guess I now have to face forever.

"I'm sorry. I'll be up in twenty minutes."

"I'd say don't bother, but we've got that big group coming in ..."

"It's fine. Don't worry. I'll be there. I'm sorry."

I look in the mirror while I brush my teeth, and see inky smudges under my eyes, red-rimmed eyes, and chapped lips. I could be a plague victim. I could be a zombie. Or a very heart-broken girl.

Being a zombie might be the least painful of those three choices.

I'm glad Betsy woke me up, because work is going to be my salvation. I'm getting stuff done, and it feels good.

I launch the vacuum cleaner across the hall runner, jabbing at a stubborn speck and, when it finally disappears, power the machine down.

In the sudden silence, I hear Betsy's voice.

"Meg! The phone's for you!" When I get to the kitchen, Betsy's holding the handset out for me.

"Meg! Are you OK? You just left yesterday. Will said you were really pale ..."

Betsy's been baking, so I wedge the phone between my ear and shoulder and run a sinkful of hot, sudsy water while I talk. "I'm fine Lace. I'm sorry I had to leave so quickly. I felt off – I don't think I'd eaten enough – I'm OK today."

"Well, I could have made you a peanut butter sandwich, you know."

I drape the measuring spoons over the edge of the draining board. "I'll keep that in mind if it ever happens again. Anyway, Lace, I probably should have called you. Are you OK? That was crazy."

"I'm better than Bridget."

"What do you mean?"

"She had a total breakdown. You should have seen it. Will found her by herself, crying out of control. She wouldn't stop no matter who talked to her. In the end, we called her mom to come pick her up, and Carly ponied Diamond back home."

"Wow. What a complete and total mess ..." It is, too. Anger doesn't even enter into it anymore. I just feel sorry for Bridget,

Lacey, Will, Jared, and me. All of us missing people we wish we could be with. None of us able to figure a way out. I sigh. "Seriously, though Lace, she really lost it on you – how are you feeling?"

She's quiet for a minute, and I wonder if she's upset, or shrugging it off. "It wasn't nice, but I try not to let it bother me. I mean, other people like me. Alanna slept over last night."

I stop myself right before I say, "I know." I don't want to have to explain how I know.

Lacey's still talking. "I don't know what's up with Bridget but I wish she'd get over it, because I really, really want to do this ride. We've worked so hard, and I'm not saying we'll win, but I think we're going to be good. Except I'm afraid the whole thing's going to fall apart now."

"Do the other girls not want to ride with her?"

"I think we all just want to move forward, but it doesn't seem like Bridget wants to."

I admire Lacey so much for her positive attitude. Especially today. I don't know how she can be so sunny.

As strong as she is, though, I also know Lacey needs my help. I might not be able to sort out my biggest problem, but maybe I can straighten out a smaller one.

I take a deep breath, release the plug from the drain, and say what I know I have to. "I'll talk to Bridget, Lace."

***

Because I missed my run this morning, I run as the sun starts to lower in the sky.

I'm doing it to tire myself out. To make sure I'll get some sleep tonight.

As I have been for a while now, I follow my old route, and run by Jared's.

It's only a couple of kilometres to his driveway but by the time I get there, my heart is hammering against my ribs, and my breath is coming short and sharp.

His truck and the tractor are in the yard.

Ohmygod, ohmygod, ohmygod. He's right there. He must be.

Rex runs out, tail wagging, and that confirms it. Jared's somewhere outside.

I crouch and open my arms, and Rex runs into them.

He knocks me flat on my back, and I don't care.

I lie and stare at the sky, and wait, and wait, and wait, and Jared doesn't come.

Rex barks at me; convinced I'm playing some silly human game, and Jared doesn't come.

Rex gives up; starts to trot away, and that's too much.

"Come back, boy!" He does, and he doesn't mind staying, once he finds the tears running down my cheeks, and realizes I'll let him lick them off.

They keep coming, though, so eventually I have to cut him off.

"That's enough, bud. You go home. Say hi to Jared. Tell him I love him."

I don't even bother to finish my route; just turn around and run the meagre two kilometres back, and when I crawl into bed I think I've never ached so much.

Chapter Twenty-Four

I *need to call Bridget.*

I can't relax on my run, or at work, or on my drive to ride Jessie.

I need to call Bridget.

Every now and then, *What am I going to do about Jared?* intrudes to distract me, but the difference is, I promised Lacey I'd call Bridget. I have an objective. I know what I have to do.

Plus, I've invested hours and weeks, and nearly two months, in training four girls for a musical ride, and I need to make sure all four are going to show up.

So, I need to call Bridget.

After work, Lacey and I take the horses out for a bareback hack.

"I'm going to call Bridget soon." I tell Lacey.

"I know you will, Meg." Her absolute trust gives me a stab of guilt at putting it off all day. I'll call from work tomorrow. Definitely. But, for now, she's also let me off the hook. Which feels nice.

We head down the driveway side-by-side. The horses' hooves clip-clop for a few seconds while we cross the highway, then we're back into the crunch-crunch of their hooves on gravel. We ride past the end of Bridget's driveway.

Lacey looks up the lane. "Meg?"

"Yeah?"

"Should I be mad at Jared?"

My heart catches. I'd rather talk about me calling Bridget. "Why do you ask?"

"I just … I heard something. A rumour. I don't want to be mad at him, but …"

"It's OK Lace. It's not worth listening to gossip. You don't need to be mad at him. He's your cousin. He's great." I don't want my voice to be so flat, but I'm afraid if I let emotion into it I'll cry.

She sits up straighter. "Can I tell him you said so?"

For the first time in days I laugh. "Lacey …"

"OK, fine. Let's ride."

At the end of the road, there's a narrow path. We give the horses their heads, and they lower their noses, and pick the best way over the rocky footing, and between overgrown shrubs.

Salem's strong, appaloosa rump works ahead of me. Lacey sits straight and tall on her back. I love that mare. Love that girl. I started loving her last year as Jared's headstrong cousin. I've come to love her this year for herself. This summer would have been much, much tougher without her.

Salem steps out onto the narrow strip of beach that was our goal, and Jessie walks up right beside her. No flattened ears; no flash of teeth. My mare's come a long way.

The horses prick their ears across the channel at Ellicott Island, but we have something else in mind.

"Come on, girl," Lacey urges. She turns Salem's head into the wind and clucks, and the mare responds willingly, jumping into a trot, and then a canter. Water sprays around her legs and splashes her belly.

Jessie jumps to attention under me. Pushes up against the bit. Snorts.

I hold her back for seconds that feel like hours to both of us. Wait until Salem passes a certain driftwood log I've chosen as a marker. Then I let her loose. "Go!"

I hope she's warmed up enough. Hope this won't hurt her. Then I let my worries go. I marvel at the thrusting power of the mare's hindquarters digging into the sand, driving us forward. I bend at my hips, leaning low against her neck, which bobs in a reach-lift-reach-lift rhythm. Her mane whips my skin, and the wind drives tears across my cheeks.

We run until the jump's gone out of the mares. Then we trot circles in the shallow water near the shore, splashing each other, sending spray into the sun.

Finally I turn Jessie straight out, and she wades into the river, ending up chest deep, taking long sucking swallows of the water.

I close my eyes, let my legs float out from her sides, and stroke her neck.

If only I could stay here forever.

***

As I drive home along the gravel road to the cottage, I watch the bars disappear on my phone. *Four, three, two ...* I brake.

What now? Call? Text? I don't know.

I scroll to Jared's name, and close my eyes. *Just do it.* I press "talk."

I hold the phone to my ear and it rings, and rings, and rings, and then I hear Jared's voice saying "Leave a message," and it almost makes me cry because of all the times I told him he needs a longer message so I could hear more of his voice when he doesn't answer.

So much for cell phones taking the mystery out of life. So much for them being the world's greatest convenience.

Because Jared's phone could be on or off. He could be right beside it, or nowhere near it. If he is near it, he might be choosing not to answer it, or have no idea it's ringing. If he does know it's ringing maybe he hates me so much he won't pick it up, or maybe he's not picking it up because he doesn't know what to say.

In other words, that call has gained me precisely no information, and given me lots to angst about, and since I hang up without leaving a message, it's not going to give Jared any information either.

So, that really didn't help.

I sigh. There's one more call I should make.

I wish I could duck out with a text, but just like with Jared last year, Adam and I have never even exchanged cell numbers, so that's out of the question.

I need to call him. Phone numbers on the island are easy to remember. They all have the same first numbers – only the last four vary – I only had to call Alanna once to know their home number off by heart. It ends in one-two-one-two.

I punch the numbers in and wait.

Ring.

I don't want to talk to Alanna.

Ring.

Don't want to talk to their dad.

Ring.

I'm nervous about talking to Adam. But I have to.

"Hello?"

"Adam!"

"Meg?"

I exhale. "Yeah, it's me."

"It's funny to hear your voice. I had this weird dream that you came by my house, but when I woke up you weren't there, so I must have imagined it."

I'm trying to read his voice. He doesn't sound angry.

"About that, Adam. I'm so sorry. I was mixed up. It was wrong. I used you to try to make myself feel better."

"And did you?" he asks.

"Did I what?"

"Did you feel better?"

I give a spluttering laugh. "I wish. I just made things worse." Then I backpedal. Fast. "Although at the beginning, that was nice ..."

"Meg ..."

"Yeah?"

"You don't have to flatter me."

I shake my head even though I know he can't see it. "I'm not. You were nice. You made me happy this summer. I'm glad I met you."

"Thanks. I'm glad I met you too."

"Really?" I ask.

"Definitely."

I straighten in the seat of the car. "That's good. I wanted to be on good terms. Because, you know, we're bound to see each other again."

"Not here," he says.

"No?"

"I'm outta here. You'll see me on TV. Or hear me on the radio."

I smile. "I can't wait Adam. You'll be great."

I still have lots of lost sleep to catch up on, so I get ready for bed as soon as I get home.

It's getting darker so much sooner these days, which reminds me the summer's drawing to a close – a whole summer without Jared – and which also makes it more tempting to climb into bed with a good book.

I've just rinsed the suds off my face when the doorbell rings.

I freeze. Nobody ever uses the doorbell here.

My parents would walk right in. Betsy, or Carl, or Jared, would knock, and call out "Hello!" as they opened the door. But … would Jared? After what's happened this summer?

Maybe he'd ring the doorbell. I peer out the bathroom window that gives onto the front porch, but I can't see as far as the door. Who designed this place, anyway?

The band keeping my hair off my face has created multiple little tufts and spikes. My skin is shiny and pink – clean, but not attractive. And my clothes – ugh, let's just say my "nice" lounging clothes are in the laundry.

The bell ding-dongs again. There's not much I can do but yank the hairband out of my hair, do some finger combing, and stand up straight so at least my posture isn't as slouchy as my t-shirt.

I come around the corner holding my breath, and as fast as I let it out because it's not Jared, I suck it back in again, because Bridget is standing there.

OK, not exactly how I'd planned to spend my evening, but I guess there's no time like the present.

Smile. She's only thirteen. You promised Lacey.

I yank the door open. "Bridget! Hi! Come on in."

She looks at me with those great big eyes, and her lip trembles, and she looks away again. "Are you sure you want me to?"

"Oh, Bridge." This cottage has seen enough tears this summer. I step forward and hug her. She really is so young; her shaking shoulders are thin and pointy under my arms. "Come on; it's not that bad."

Her mom's standing on the ground, beside their car. *Do you want to come in?* I mouth.

She shakes her head. I read her lips. *In a bit.* She points up the driveway. *I'll walk first.*

When I get Bridget inside her cheeks are wet. "Hot chocolate?" I ask.

"Yes, please."

"It'll just take a minute."

We listen to the whirring of the microwave. I wait for her to explain why she came. The microwave beeps, and she still hasn't said anything.

I carry our mugs into the living room and point for her to sit beside me on the big, soft couch. We put our feet on the coffee table, and stare out at the moon silvering the river.

It's actually easier this way, not facing each other. No eye contact to worry about. "So. What's up?"

She sighs. "I'm sorry. I said so many things I shouldn't have. I told my mom, and she was so mad at me. I hurt Lacey's feelings. And your feelings. And W ..." Her breath comes in sharp little hiccups. "... W-W-W-Will."

"You know, Lacey and Will are really nice people. I'm sure you can make it up to them."

She sniffs. "Will said he never wanted to talk to me again. He said I was selfish and horrible. He said I used being sick as an excuse to be mean to people."

She turns to me. "I didn't, you know. At least, that's not what I meant to do. Everyone thought being sick was hard, and fighting to get better was brave, but it wasn't. That part was really straightforward. It was after, when everyone was calling me 'Wonder Girl,' and they expected so much from me."

"I never thought it could be easy being a Wonder Girl."

"That's just the thing. It was simple when it was just going for treatment and not complaining, but when all that was done, I had no idea how to be special anymore. What's special about some thirteen-year-old girl who's just like any other thirteen-year-old girl, except she doesn't have hair? I guess I just wanted to be *noticed.*"

How can I judge her? I'm the one who stood outside on the porch right here, and told Jared I wanted him to show me he cared.

It's not so different. In fact, it's hardly different at all. I clear my throat, and Bridget continues.

"I know, I know … my mom's already told me … I was getting noticed in the wrong way. I even knew it at the time. And then the worst thing was, at the dance, even that loser turned me down." She sits up straight and a bit of the old Bridget spirit resurfaces. "I mean, I'm way smarter than him, and all he talks about are these boring video game commentaries he watches on YouTube, and he had the nerve to take off with his friends and tell me I couldn't come."

I look away so she won't see me smile. Hearing that he rejected Bridget is the first thing I've actually liked about that guy.

"Anyway, by Wednesday I was so mad. And Lacey is always so cheerful and perfect … sometimes she's hard to be friends with. I felt like making everybody miserable with me. So I did."

Familiar again. Except I don't have Bridget's defence of being thirteen. I take a deep breath. "Believe it or not, I get it Bridget. I do understand."

"I'm sorry, Meg. My mom said you probably felt like people were talking about you behind your back. It wasn't like that, I swear. I didn't even know anything about it until I was talking to my sister a little while ago, and said you were my coach. She asked if you had a boyfriend, and I said I heard you broke up at the beginning of the summer, and she said it might be her fault. I was mad at her when she told me. But then, when I was having such a bad day, it seemed like the perfect thing to throw at you." She takes my arm. "I promise, promise, promise I won't say anything to anybody else."

I pull my legs up on the sofa and turn to face her. I shake my finger and hope I look serious. "Yeah, well, make sure you don't.

Not just because it's about me, but because I don't want to have riders who gossip in my musical ride and, Bridget, I'd like you to stay in the ride."

"Really?" I didn't know eyes could go as round as hers do. "I'd like to as well, but what about the others? What about Will?"

I bite my lip. "Yeah, that's going to be tricky. You need to make an effort; to show the other girls you're committed to being a good friend, and you're committed to the ride. And I think if you do that, Will is going to notice."

She throws her hands up in the air. "How, though? What do I do?"

I shake my head. "That part's up to you, Bridget. It doesn't have to be heroic, but you do need to reach out to them – to make the first move. If you don't do anything, you'll end your summer lonely, instead of with your friends, doing this ride we've all spent so much time training for."

"Yoo-hoo! Hello?" Bridget's mom is back from her walk.

"Come in! Do you want a drink?"

She walks into the living room and perches on a chair near us. "No thank you. It's getting late, and we shouldn't keep you any longer, Meg. I hope you two had a good talk."

I nod. "I was about to tell Bridget that Will's offered to hay the front field and mark out a space the exact size of the ring at the fair. He's going to do that on Saturday, so we're going to have a special practice on Sunday to do a complete run-through of the routine. No horses – just us walking everything through until we know the patterns cold. I'm hoping Bridget can make it."

Her mom looks at her, and Bridget gives a tiny nod. Then she nods again, more sharply, and says, "Yes. I'll be there."

"Excellent."

I walk them to the end of the porch. Bridget's mom goes ahead down the stairs and Bridget hesitates for a moment. "I'll think about what you said, Meg. About making the first move. I'm going to try."

Back inside, I carry our hot chocolate mugs to the sink and rinse them out.

My eyes settle on the delicate pendant and snapped chain still in their dish on the windowsill.

If I don't do something to make things right with Jared, I'll never have a reason to fix them.

I dip my finger in the dish, stir the silver links with my finger tip, and think about making the first move.

Chapter Twenty-Five

While working for Betsy I've learned vinegar will clean almost anything. I've learned that almost any tense situation can be diffused with a smile and an offer of a cup of tea. And I've also learned that ironing can be very soothing.

Or, at least that's what she told me when she taught me how to iron duvet covers. Later on, Carl let it slip that Betsy absolutely despises ironing.

I really don't mind it, though, and as I work the wrinkles out of the first of a stack of pillow shams, my mind jumps to making the first move.

I wince. I'm the one who told Jared I expected a grand gesture; now it seems like it might be up to me to deliver one.

How? Now I know how Bridget feels. Now I know how Jared must have felt all summer.

Saying sorry so that people know you mean it is hard.

I move steadily through the pile of ironing while the sun moves higher in the sky, and my stomach starts to growl, and I'm no closer to settling on my first move.

All I know for sure is that calling Jared's cell phone, and not leaving messages, doesn't count.

Betsy comes into the kitchen and starts pulling out lunch ingredients. "Egg salad?" she asks. "With a pickle on the side?"

"Perfect."

"Now, unplug that iron and have your lunch and, I'll pour you a lemonade."

"Betsy, do you mind if I use the computer while I eat?"

"Not at all. Help yourself."

"Thanks." I pick up my plate, and my glass of lemonade, and head for the den. Now the hard work begins.

I give myself fifteen minutes to figure out what to say to Jared. I do better with deadlines.

I login, open a fresh message, and there's so much white staring at me, with invitations to Add a Subject and Add a Message. Oh sure, I'll just "add" one – why didn't I think of that?

Just write the truth.

Dear Jared. I'm so sorry for everything I've done, and everything that's happened. I'm sorry for the summer we haven't spent together.

Keep going.

I miss you. This is the loneliest I've ever been. Nothing is the same without you, and nobody is the same as you.

Eleven minutes left.

I know I said you ruined everything. I think I was wrong. It hurt at first to realize things couldn't stay the way they used to be. But thinking of being without you forever hurts more. I'd rather have a different future, with you, than sit around and think about the past.

And?

I've grown up this summer. I've learned things that I think could make us better than before, if you're willing to give it a chance.
Please say yes.
I love you.
I do.
I hope you still love me, too.
xo, Meg

My finger hovers over the message options.

Not cancel. Not that. I don't know if it's the best message ever written, but it's true. It's how I feel. So I can't imagine doing better than that.

Not send either. An email is *not* a grand gesture.

Instead I choose Print. The printer whirs and clicks and, for once, there's enough paper, and no paper jam, and ink in the cartridge – all good omens? – and I scoop the printed sheet up, fold it three times, and shove it into my back pocket.

"Meg?" I turn to see Betsy standing in the doorway.

"Yes? Sorry, have you been standing there long? I was in my own world ..."

"I was just offering you this." She holds out a brownie on a plate. "It's the last one."

I look at it for a minute. Then look up at her. "Sure, why not? Gotta seize opportunities, right?"

"That's the spirit."

I nibble a corner off my brownie. "Speaking of which – do you know where I could get some really nice writing paper?"

***

I turn back from getting a Diet Coke out of the fridge, and am confronted with the cottage table.

Oh my gosh. Did I do that?

Two empty cans of Diet Coke. A scraped-clean pot with faint remnants of Kraft Dinner and ketchup around the edges. The ketchup bottle. And paper. Paper everywhere. With hand-writing on it. Bold handwriting. Tentative handwriting. Cursive. Print. Crossed-out. Crumpled up.

Somewhere in the middle of that is my original document. The one I printed off at Betsy's today. Also somewhere in there must be my Kraft Dinner fork. Which is a bit worrying …

Kept safe on the sideboard are the precious sheets of thick, creamy writing paper Betsy handed over to me before I left work. I only have two left.

Time to get serious. Dirty dishes go to the sink. Empty cans to recycling. Each discarded attempt – both the practice ones on printer paper, and the couple I've already screwed up on Betsy's nice paper – goes in a stack.

Now I have a clear space. Now I have the note to copy from spread in front of me. Now I'm holding the pen that doesn't blot, or bleed. Now the pressure's on.

I sit back, turn my head sideways, and squint. The big picture, soft-focus effect is good enough. Even hand-writing. Most words legible.

I read it over again word by word, out loud to make sure I haven't done something stupid like leave out an "and." I better not have. I don't have the energy to go back and start from scratch.

OK. It's done. It's as good as I'm going to make it. I fold it exactly in half, lining the edges up before I press down on the crease. I scrawl *Jared* in bold letters on the envelope, then I slide the note in and prop it on the shelf by the front door.

The sun's just rolling up above the horizon when I start my morning run. I have the precious envelope in a Ziploc bag to protect it from sweaty fingerprints.

I spent all night picturing this delivery, so that it worked its way into my dreams, and I imagined chasing Jared's retreating truck and never quite being able to catch it. Trying to reach Jared but being stopped by a bull. Or a pack of coyotes. Or, once, by Adam.

I don't think I want to see Jared. I mean, I do, but only after he's read the note and had time to think about it. Only once I'll be able to see where I stand.

Maybe not handing it to him directly is common sense, or maybe it's a defense mechanism. A cop out. A sign of weakness. I don't know.

It might also just be practicality. There's a good chance I won't see Jared this morning, and I have to get this envelope out of my custody so I can stop thinking about it.

I have a plan.

Rex runs out to greet me before I even reach the driveway. I've brought a treat for him, and he's more than happy to take it from me and sit, and have his neck rubbed, and his ears scratched.

"You need to do me a favour, bud."

He turns his head sideways, and with his one ear that points, and one that's always floppy, he looks just like he's listening to me.

The Ziploc bag wasn't just for protection against my fingers. I've reinforced the plastic at the top of the bag with tape, and punched two holes through it. I fish two zip ties out of my shorts pocket, and thread one through each of the holes, and then around Rex's collar.

All last night I wondered where to leave the envelope. Jared might not go into the house all day. Plus, his mom would see it. The barn's so big that no matter where I left it, he might not find it. And I didn't want to get caught sneaking into his truck with it parked right outside the house. But Rex is perfect. Rex is Jared's shadow. Jared will definitely see Rex. And he loves Rex, so maybe he'll be more kindly disposed toward a note brought by his dog. I would be.

I give Rex a final ear rub. "Off you go! Go see Jared!"

It's out of my hands now. Literally.

I head back home to get ready for work.

Did I really think that sending the letter off with Rex would make me stop thinking about it?

The complete opposite has happened. I should have attached a GPS tracker to the envelope because then I could see where it is, instead of imagining half a dozen possibilities: still on Rex's collar while he snoozes in the sun. Ripped off and stuck on a branch of a bush. Dropped on the pile of mail Jared's mom always leaves by the kitchen door. In Jared's back pocket.

Mmm ... Jared's back pocket ...

"Meg!"

I nearly drop the bag of sugar I'm using to fill the sugar bowl. "What?"

"What are you doing?" Betsy asks.

"Filling the sugar bowl."

"That's salt," she says.

"Oh, whoops."

"Why are you so distracted? I found the fruit bowl in the refrigerator. I don't even know how you got it to fit in there."

"Sorry. I've got a lot on my mind. The musical ride run-through's tomorrow ... but I'll focus, Betsy. I will."

"Why don't you go clean out the chicken coop? Maybe some fresh air will help."

I clean and feed the chickens, then stand in the quiet of the coop, with the sunlight filtering in, watching the hypnotic pecking of the chickens.

I go back into the house, refreshed and ready to work.

I'm halfway up the stairs when Betsy's voice floats up behind me. "Meg! You left the door wide open!"

It's going to be one of those days.

I keep waiting for Jared to charge in and tell Betsy he needs to talk to me right away, and say that he wants us to be together forever again, effective immediately.

He doesn't, though.

I'm rapidly losing my dignity. On my way to riding, I detour off the highway and drive by Jared's.

I'm not proud of it, but I need to see if he's there. What he might be doing. If I can learn anything.

It's quiet. His truck's not in the yard. Rex is nowhere in sight.

Information gathered: zero.

Will's on the tractor when I arrive at Lacey's. "I'm nearly done that field for tomorrow," he says.

"Thanks. It should be great. I really appreciate it."

"Um, Meg ... Lacey said you were going to talk to Bridget."

"Yup. I did. She said she's coming tomorrow."

Will nods. "OK. Good to know."

I wonder whether to say more. Don't know what I'd say, though. Will and Bridget's relationship – whatever it is – is between Will and Bridget. And Will's not asking, anyway.

"Is Lacey around?" I ask.

"No. She's gone to Carly's, I think. Or she and Carly are at Alanna's. I can't remember, but they're all off together."

"Thanks."

I go catch Jessie. "Just you and me this evening, girl."

I take her into the ring; work through a nice, long, bending, flexing warm-up. But my mind's not with it. I can't think what to do next. There's nothing I really want to work on. Our swim with Lacey and Salem was so nice.

I scratch her withers. "Wanna go on a hack?"

We head the opposite direction from the other day. Turn right on the first concession road we get to, then strike off along a worn path away from that road. There's an old quarry back here. I'd love to see it.

The light's already gone golden and the shadows are long. For the last couple of weeks I've felt like I can count the minutes of daylight shortening.

There's a rustling behind us, and one to the side. Jessie switches to high alert; ears swiveling, nostrils flared, and a light tremble running under the skin of her neck.

"It's OK. Easy girl. It's fine." I nudge her forward. Keeping her walking, under my command, is the best thing I can do. If I let her stop, there's no telling how explosive her movement will be once it comes.

Her steps are stiff and halting, and her neck is right up in my face. "Come on, sweetie. Walk on."

Then, *Boom!* One deer, two deer, three deer, materialize from the undergrowth. They leap away from us, bouncing on pogo legs, white tails held high and flashing through the grainy early evening light.

Jessie's had enough. Her quarter horse hocks coil under her and spring us both forward, and we're running, belting, fleeing – first on the path and then, when we round a corner and face another deer right in front of us, off it.

The uneven footing breaks her long strides into ragged staggers. *OK, this is fine.* I should be able to stop her. I sit back, sink my heels low, and open my mouth to say, "Whoa!"

She slams to a halt. I still haven't said anything. Still haven't given her the sharp half-halt I was preparing.

I'm glad she's stopped, but it's weird.

Her sides are heaving, and she's still twitching, but that's the only movement she makes. She doesn't shift, or side-step. She doesn't back up or step forward.

I look down.

Oh no.

Barbed wire.

Coiled around her legs.

I can't tell how bad it is, or how high it goes. Whether it's touching her belly. If her hind legs are in it. I have to find out.

Which means I have to dismount. Which I'm terrified to do, because what if my getting off makes her move? Also, there's the small question of how I dismount without ending up in wire myself.

"What a mess."

Her ears turn to my voice. She needs me. I have to help her. I smooth my hand down her neck. "It's OK. We'll get you out of here."

I keep talking, saying senseless things. Lots of "It's OK. It's alright. It'll be fine."

I babble as I shift in the saddle and as I choose the side with less wire on it: her off, right side. Not the proper side to dismount from, but the side I might be able to land on, wire free.

I sing a song as I bunch my legs under me for leverage and say, "Whoa! Stand!" right before I propel myself off with a huge push from my arms and legs. I land on all fours, with the sole of my boot touching wire, and twist to see every muscle of my sweet, brave mare tensed, but she hasn't moved.

"Good girl."

I circle her. "Good girl, easy girl, stand girl."

Because she was smart enough to stop, it's OK right now. There are a couple of places in her front legs where the wire's nicked her, but there are no snarling tangles; no gushing blood. Her hind end is clear and, if I step carefully, I can reach her head. It could have been worse but, there's still enough to cut deep into her skin and do lasting damage, if she panics.

I can't do this alone. I don't have gloves, let alone wire-cutters. I need help.

We're far from the closest house, and I can't leave her anyway. I need to stay here and make sure nothing happens to make her move.

Whoever comes has to be somebody she trusts. I don't want a stranger crashing through the bushes, freaking her out; convincing her to take her chances with the wire to get away from them.

I pull out my phone. *Please be charged. Please let me have a signal.*

Jessie trusts Lacey. But Lacey can't drive, and I'm probably better with wire cutters than she is.

His name is at the top of my recent contacts. Please let him have a signal. Please let him answer.

One ring. Two rings. Three and four, and, just when I'm about to give up, the voice I've wanted to hear. "I'm on my way now."

For a minute I believe he's telepathic. We're *that* meant for each other. He's sensed my distress, and is heading my way. Then I snap out of it. "What? How can you be?"

"Your letter. I'm coming."

The words I've wanted to hear – longed to hear – and my fear won't let me savour them. "I'm not at home. I'm with Jessie. She needs you. We need you. *I* need you, Jared. I really, really need you."

"I'll be there as fast as I can," was the last thing he said. I know he will, but he's still halfway across the island.

That's going to take a while.

"So, it's you and me, Jess. What are we going to do? How are we going to keep you happy?"

I stroke her neck, and my mouth's getting dry from talking, but I keep it up anyway.

She shifts, and I freeze. I get it. She has to shift her weight. But if she moves her legs ... I shudder.

"Let's try this."

I let her reins dangle to the ground. Out of habit I unbuckle them so she won't catch her leg in them. The reins seem like the least of our concerns right now.

We've practiced ground-tying before; I just hope she remembers it now. I walk to her rump, take hold of her tail, and she turns to look at me. She knows what comes next.

I move into our massage routine, working all her big muscles, then switching sides. She stands, good as gold, and, eventually stretches her neck out low, letting her head hang and her lip droop.

I massage her until my hand tingles and my arms are heavy with the effort. I rub her hide while the sun sets, and the evening sounds start up, and I pray for no more deer to come crashing into our space. A mosquito whines in my ear, and I pray for the onslaught of bugs to hold off. My arm goes numb, and I pray to not have to do this for too much longer.

He comes carefully. He comes talking. He comes calling her name and mine.

"Hey Meg-and-Jessie. Hey my two girls. How are you girls?"

Jessie lifts her head but easily, calmly. One ear stays on me; the other swivels to Jared's voice. She's paying attention; not panicking. Thank goodness.

"We're here. Can you find us?"

"Keep talking."

"Follow the path for a bit, then you'll probably see where we crashed off it."

"I think I see it. Is she OK?"

"She hears you coming. She's staying calm."

"Hey Jess-Jess-Jess. Hey silly."

She whickers.

If I ever doubted that Jared was a good guy – the right guy – there can't be any doubt left when my sensitive little mare calls to him like that. When he steps into our clearing, and relief nearly takes my knees out from under me. "Thank God you're here."

"Are you OK?" Jared asks.

I'd forgotten how those words, when Jared says them to me in that tone of voice, mean the same as *I'm going to make you OK.*

"I am now." Just on edge, and trying not to let my edginess seep through to my horse.

It's nearly dark. Hard to see. I put my hand out and it hits Jared's arm. Warm. Strong. "Be careful. I don't know if you can see all the wire in this light."

His hand covers mine for just a second. Then he squeezes and lets go so he can swing a backpack to the ground. "Here. I brought these." He pulls two headlamps from the pocket.

I snug mine around my forehead. "Please tell me you have wire cutters in there."

He holds them up, and they shine dully in the beams of our headlamps.

Jessie's on alert again. Horses shouldn't be out, without their herd, in the dark. Her instincts know that. She's still waiting for us, but her ears are at attention and her breathing's quickened.

"Jared, she's ..."

"I know. The thing is, Meg, you never know where this stuff is going to go when you cut. It doesn't just fall away. It'll bounce and recoil."

He's right. I shudder. "So, how do we handle that?"

He reaches into the bag again. "I brought shipping bandages. I thought it might help to wrap her legs first, before we start cutting."

Genius.

"What's that?"

"You're a complete genius." I'm already on my knees by Jessie's hind end, wrapping those legs just in case. They aren't the most even bandages ever put on a horse, but I'm in a hurry, and they're protection.

The forelegs are going to be much harder. To wrap them I have to get close.

Jared stands by Jessie's head and strokes her cheek, and shines his lamp down on the wire. "How about there? That strand?" He nods to highlight the one he means. "If you put your boot on that, can you get close enough to lean in and wrap her?"

"I'll try."

I have to thread my arms through strands of wire, but I manage it. We work together, Jared talking me through the job, me wrapping. They're the sloppiest bandages of my riding career, but who cares? They're covering thin skin and valuable ligaments, tendons, and muscle. When I touch her legs Jessie twitches, but lets me wrap her. She's getting "good girl" in stereo from both Jared and me.

I stand up.

"Nice job." Jared says.

"Great idea."

It's a good thing it's too dark for eye-gazing, because we don't have time for that, but it's so tempting.

"Now for the cutting." I move to take Jared's place at Jessie's head.

"Meg ..."

"What?"

He reaches out and strokes my cheek with his thumb. For a second, I'm not rushed or scared. A tremble runs through my jaw, and shivers out my shoulders. He holds his thumb between us, and it's smeared with blood. "You're cut."

"Oh." I put my fingers to my cheek. "I didn't feel it." I shake my head. "Let's keep going."

The first couple of cuts are easy. Jared chooses pieces of wire farther away from Jess; working his way in to the ones tightest to her legs.

Jessie doesn't like it. Even though it's Jared down there, every snip sets her on edge. I place my body against her head, and she pushes into me, hard. She stamps her front foot and I suck my breath in.

"It's OK," Jared says. "She just lifted it straight up and down. It didn't catch."

We're running out of time.

"What'll happen if you let go of her head?" he asks.

"Why?"

"I want you to hold one side of this wire. I'll try to hold the other side while I cut so it doesn't fly away and hit her. There's another pair of gloves in the pack."

I ground-tie Jess again, order "Whoa," put on the gloves, and squat by Jared.

"Hold there. I'll cut here."

He's holding the cutters in one hand, holding the wire with his other.

"This is stupid. You need both hands." I reach around him for the other side of the wire. Now I'm jammed halfway under my horse's belly, straddling my ex-boyfriend. I press my head against his back, and it rises and falls with the open and close of his ribcage as he breathes. As he works to get my horse free.

"I love you." I breathe it on an exhale, as he inhales. For a tiny second the in-and-out rhythm of his ribs pauses. Everything's still. Then he reaches for another strand of wire. Except, he pushes back against me first, ever-so-slightly.

He continues – *snip, hold, point, snip, hold, point* – and I contribute a steady stream of, "Whoa, Jessie," and "Good girl."

And then: "Done."

"What?"

"That's it. She's free."

"She's ..." Before I can say anything else, a massive shudder runs through Jessie's body.

"Hold down the loose wire!" Jared warns, and not a minute too soon, because the mare does a sort of mini-levade, and pivots, before crow-hopping forward a couple of times.

I jump up. "Easy girl." I walk toward her, palms forward. "Whoa. Just wait there."

She doesn't wait. She reaches her nose out and steps forward, and I expect her to be trembling, but it's me; I'm the one shaking.

And then, steadying me, are hands on my shoulders. Jared presses his thumbs against my shoulder blades, pulls my shoulders back and down, and tension I didn't know I was holding evaporates as the words I've been waiting for come, "I love you, too."

"Mmmm ..." I lean back, loll my head to the side, and shiver as his lips trail up my neck, brushing my ear lobe, then back down again.

He circles his arms around me, and whispers, "Turn around," and I do, staying inside his arms, ending up facing him in the dark. I study his eyes, glowing in the reflected moonlight, but don't rest there for long. My gaze travels to his lips, slightly cracked, lightly chapped, parted just a bit, then I reach to trace my fingertips along his moon-highlighted cheek bones.

To have Jared right in front of me – the warmth of his body pressing the length of mine; his skin, lightly stubbled, under the pads of my fingers – it's quickening my breath, and my pulse. Making me dizzy and lightheaded, and sending a fizzing weakness through my hips, legs, knees.

He presses his fingers to my lips, tracing their outline, pressing on my bottom lip with his thumb. I instinctively open my mouth wider, and then his lips are on mine – soft at first – so, so soft. Teasing, and nibbling, until a rush of longing tingles through me, and I push my lips against his, and we're kissing, kissing, kissing, and it's more frantic, and even better than our first kiss ever – the one I've socked away to hold onto forever because I thought nothing could ever match it.

We kiss like that for I don't know how long, gasping for air, hands finding each other's hair and ears and necks – anything to grab onto, to pull each other closer. He circles his arms behind me and finds my lower back and pulls, and I'm afraid I can't stop, don't want to stop, but I know I have to stop, and how am I ever going to stop, and then a draft of warm breath gusts across both our necks.

I giggle, and pull back. "Jess!"

Jared props his forehead against mine. "Whose idea was it to bring the horse?"

I laugh again. "I missed you."

"I missed *that*."

"*That* was just the beginning."

"Is that a promise?"

"That's a promise … except for one thing."

"Oh yeah, the horse."

"Yup. Let's get her home."

I hold my hand out, and he threads his fingers through mine, and Jessie walks behind us, with her bobbing nose brushing our interlaced hands.

Chapter Twenty-Six

In the morning I'm not jumping up and down, or dancing, or singing out loud – although I might possibly hum a bit. I'm brimming with quiet happiness.

I'm satisfied.

My heart quickens when there's a knock on the B&B door and Betsy goes to open it. I take a break from chopping fruit for the guests, and listen. "Oh, Jared. I'm surprised you didn't see Carl. He was working in the garage, but maybe he's gone around back …"

"Actually, I came to see Meg. If that's OK."

"Of course. Come in to the kitchen."

By the time he walks around the corner, I'm grinning so hard my cheeks hurt. "Hi."

"Hi."

I've missed saying hi to him, and hearing it back, so I say it again. "Hi."

"Hi."

"Oh my goodness," Betsy says, and walks out of the room. She doesn't go far though; I know because the floor only creaks under her feet a few times.

I lift my chopping board. "Want some pineapple? Freshly sliced."

"I can't stay. I came to say I'll pick you up after work to go get your car, if you like."

It's part of the reason I left my car at Lacey's last night, after we got Jessie settled, and accepted a drive home from Jared. I wanted him to have to drive me back today.

"Yes, please."

"And also to ask if you'd come for dinner tonight? My mom wants you to."

"Your mom?"

He nods.

"You told her?"

"She saw me smiling. She figured it out."

I'm smiling too. "Yes, I'd love to come. Please tell her thanks for the invitation."

He hasn't been gone for ten seconds before Betsy's back. Her eyes are gleaming. "Meg, honestly, I couldn't be happier."

"Yeah, well, that makes two of us."

***

When we get to Lacey's, Will's running around the hayed field clutching – and dropping – dressage letters, with Lacey yelling at him to tell him where they go, and Alanna watching them from a few steps back.

I tap Alanna on the back. "Come with me."

"What?"

We start walking to the barn. "Jessie had an adventure last night. I want to see how she's doing."

She already has her head stuck over the gate, with Jared feeding her carrots. "I'm no expert, but she looks good," he says.

"Let's take her in."

While Alanna grooms her, I run my hands down her legs. Cool, firm. A few healing cuts, but everything dry. Nothing bleeding or weeping.

"She seems fine." I raise my eyebrows at Jared. "Thanks to you."

He bows. "I'm not going to argue."

"Lacey said we're not riding, so do you just want me to turn her out again?" Alanna asks.

"Do you mind hand-walking her for five or ten minutes? Just to stretch her legs out and see how she looks?"

"Of course not." Alanna clucks Jessie forward, and the mare goes with her happily. The list of people Jessie trusts is getting longer every day.

I meet Lacey on the driveway. "Hey! Jessie looks good, doesn't she?" Before I can answer, she points toward the road. "Carly's here!"

Sure enough, solid old Shelby is walking along, carrying Carly.

I shade my hand against the sun and squint. "Someone else, too."

"Bridget?" Lacey asks.

"Yep. You good with that?"

She tilts her head and wrinkles her nose. "Yeah. I want to do this ride. We need her. It'll be fine."

When the two girls ride up, I work hard at greeting Bridget and Carly in exactly the same voice, as if I never doubted, for even one second, that Bridget would show up. I pretend I'm absolutely positive she's going to be cheerful, positive, and polite today.

"I wasn't planning on using the horses today," I say.

Bridget shrugs. "I know, but this way we didn't need a drive. We'll just leave them in the sand ring until we're ready to go back."

It's one thing to treat Bridget's arrival as no big deal. I still have one very big deal ahead of me: going through the entire ride, once and for all. Seeing if the individual circles, and serpentines, and cross throughs we've been working on for nearly two months flow together and look good enough to impress an audience, while being simple enough that the girls can get through them all moving well, with no mistakes.

I meet Jared's eyes and he winks, and that makes everything so much easier. If Jared and I figured out our problems, this should be a cinch.

"Carly, since you have him here anyway, can I borrow Shelby?" I say.

I cross Carly's stirrups over Shelby's withers and gather up my reins, when Bridget interrupts. "Wait, Meg."

Everyone stares at me, and I hold my breath. *What now?*

"I have something you might want to use. I mixed the music. It's the right length – all ready to go."

Oh. "Great Bridget. Thanks. Can you hand it to Will, and he can play it for me?"

One point for Bridget.

The music starts and I begin the routine with it.

I ride and talk. While I'm riding one circle, I gesture to the other side of the ring, "… and Lacey will be over there, and Bridget will be in that corner …" While I'm crossing the diagonal, I call, "Remember, Alanna will be coming the opposite direction." I urge Shelby through a serpentine. I put him in his spot as the pivot of the wheel, which looks less-than-spectacular. I finish on the centre line and drop my head. Will cuts the music, and I look up.

"So?"

Lacey's first. "It's awesome! And the music was perfect."

Then Alanna says, "I really think we can do it."

Carly's eyes are huge. "Shelby looked so good."

I laugh. "About that. Can I just say you must have amazing legs? He is *so* hard to keep moving."

She blushes. "Thanks."

Bridget still hasn't said anything. I look at her. "Well?"

"It's good. It's great. But it's still missing something …" She looks even more adorable than when I first met her. Her eyes are still huge in her small face, but now the fuzz growing all over her head is starting to curl. I brace for attitude.

Her eyes sparkle and her mouth breaks into a wide smile. "Don't you think, girls?"

I look around, and realize Carly and Alanna are racing back along the path. "What's going on?"

Lacey shrugs. "No idea." I don't blame her for the frown on her face, or the furrow between her brows.

Bridget turns to us. "Trust us, guys. We have something to show you. Just wait on the side. She looks over at Jared and Will.

"With the boys." There's a tease in her voice when she says "Boys" and Will's cheeks flush bright red.

I stand beside Jared. "Did Will say anything? Do you know what's going on?"

"No clue."

Carly and Alanna are leading Diamond back now. They halt him at a spot in front of us, and Bridget grabs Lacey's hand. "Come on."

Lacey hesitates. Bridget tugs, and both girls look at me.

"Go," I tell Lacey.

Bridget positions Lacey beside Diamond, then gives a hand signal, and the horse extends one foreleg, bends the other, and lowers his head to his knee.

"Oh my ..." I'd almost forgotten about Diamond's trick background.

"Get up!" Bridget tells Lacey.

"What? Me?"

"Yes, you. Get on him."

Lacey steps forward slowly, swings her leg over his back, and shifts to adjust herself in the saddle.

"Get ready!" Bridget says, and gives another signal, and Diamond raises back up.

Lacey looks at Jared and me, and her eyes are round; mouth open.

I clap. "Nice job, Lace!"

"Are you a good boy, Diamond?" Bridget asks, and the horse stretches his nose forward and nods his head several times. All the girls are giggling.

Now Bridget steps to Lacey's side and says something I can't hear. Lacey shakes her head. Bridget nods, and Carly says, "Go for it!" and, next thing I know, Lacey shrugs, drops Diamond's reins across his withers, pulls her legs up under her, and starts to stand up.

"No ..." I squeeze Jared's arm.

"It's OK. She's fine."

Lacey bobbles, and Bridget holds a hand up for her. Lacey's chest rises and falls, and she stands the rest of the way up.

"Alright! Now for the finale!"

I hold my breath. What does Bridget mean? She'd better not make Diamond rear with Lacey balanced on his back. I'm braced to run forward when Diamond lifts his head and whinnies, long and loud.

Shelby, Salem, and Jessie all answer back, and I laugh, and clap, and when I look at Lacey she's wearing the biggest smile I've ever seen on her. Which is a very big smile indeed.

After we've walked through the routine three more times on foot, and the girls have asked questions, I hand out copies for them to study at home. "Remember: you can work through bits of it if you're schooling at home, but don't put it all together because we don't want the horses starting to anticipate the moves."

Will asks Jared to look at a sticking trailer hitch, and I bring Jessie back in to mist her legs again.

I crouch beside the mare, and spray saline on her healing cuts, and listen to the conversation taking place just outside the barn doors as all four girls practice braiding on Shelby and Diamond.

"That was the best."

"That was so cool."

"We should definitely win with that move at the end of our routine."

"When did you guys plan that?" I recognize Lacey's voice.

Carly answers. "Bridget called us and we went over to her place a couple of times. She said she wanted to make sure we had a great finale, and she wanted it to be a surprise."

I straighten to run the soft brush over Jessie's coat again and gaze out the doors. Lacey's facing Bridget. "But he's your horse. You should be on him for his tricks."

Bridget shakes her head. "You made this happen, Lacey. If you hadn't organized it, we wouldn't be doing this. You have to be our finale rider."

"I ..."

Carly chips in. "Definitely." And Alanna nods. "I agree."

Bridget looks up, and meets my eyes, and I nod and mouth, *Awesome job.*

And then Jared and Will appear, and I figure they must have heard everything, and I think Bridget should be well on her way back into Will's good books.

I drive my car back home, but Jared insists on picking me up for dinner. "I'll come get you in an hour," he says.

"You don't have to."

"I want to. It's like a date." He scrunches his nose. "Except with my mom."

"I love your mom."

Because it's a kind-of date, I jump in the river, and wash my hair, and put on a swishy skirt, and a t-shirt I've never worn to ride in.

Once I'm ready, I wait for Jared on the porch, and he whistles when he rolls down the window. He reaches for the door handle and I run down the stairs.

"Don't bother getting out. Really. I'm nervous and I just want to get in the truck and get over there."

"Why on earth are you nervous? My mom loves you. Besides, you've had dinner at my house a hundred times."

We're rumbling down the driveway now and I turn to him. "Oh, come on, Jared."

"OK, I get it. I just don't want you to worry."

"I won't, once we're sitting down. I know it'll be fine. It just feels ... symbolic."

He reaches over and taps my shoulder. "That's because it is. It's a symbol that she's as glad as I am to have you around again."

"Don't get me wrong; I'm glad to be going."

"Then we're all glad. Which is good."

Jared's mom hugs me as soon as I step in the door. She's made all my favourite food. Rex even sleeps across my feet as I eat.

Jared's telling his mom about Bridget's surprise stunt move, when she puts down her fork.

"I'm sorry to interrupt, but can I just say something?"

Jared and I look at each other. "Sure."

"Can I just tell you how many times all summer I wanted to shake both of you?"

"Mom!"

"It's OK, Jared," I say. "I know what she means. I wanted to shake you, too."

He grins. "Oh, I wasn't trying to get her to stop talking; I just wanted to make sure she knew it was mostly your fault."

His mom picks up her napkin and flicks it at his head. "For God's sake Jared, I've missed this girl. You be nice to her, or I'll kick you out and ask her to move in."

It feels good to climb into Jared's truck for the drive home. When we get there he parks, hops out and walks with me to the front door. This time I don't try to stop him.

"You coming in?"

"You want me to?"

I stand on my tiptoes and nuzzle my face against his neck. Whisper, "Definitely."

He comes in.

He closes the door behind us with one hand, while circling me with the other. I slide the leftover pie his mom sent home onto the kitchen counter, leaving both my hands free to go around his waist.

I take his bottom lip between my teeth and pull it, gently, and he pushes into me, kissing me back twice as hard, sliding his hand under my bum and lifting me toward the stairs.

I start climbing them, backward, one at a time. *Step-shuffle-kiss. Step-shuffle-kiss.* Until we hit the top and I stumble back, tripping over my t-shirt on the floor, over my own feet, landing on my bed with him falling on top of me.

He's warm and heavy; not in a hurting way, but in a delicious, solid way. I reach down and find the hem of his t-shirt and yank. It comes up, sticks on his chin, and I pull harder, until it's free; until his skin is bare under my hands. But it's not enough. I wriggle and squirm under him, working my own shirt up, pulling it over my head between kisses.

There's nothing like this – lying skin-to-skin with Jared again. He trails his hand down my side and a shudder runs through me.

And then I'm lost. Lost in his kisses, and the warmth of him so close to me, and – even while I'm enjoying every sensation – a part of me is pulling back; seeing us from some objective distance. Two people who love each other, on a soft bed, under cottagey eaves, surrounded by the moon-silvered river, and the starlit fields, on an island we both love.

It's perfect, and I treasure it more because of the work we had to do to get here.

There were times this summer when I thought I'd never have this with Jared again, and now I do. A shiver of bliss seizes me right down to my toes, and Jared laughs. "What are you doing?"

"I'm just so happy."

"Mmm ... he nuzzles his head against my neck, and I relax against him. I lie and stare at the high-peaked ceiling, and am reminded of that wide world around us by the howl of a coyote drifting through the window, and the low engine rumble of a Laker far out in the shipping channel. I run my fingers through the not-curly, not-straight hair I love so much.

Jared stirs and mumbles something about his mom.

"Why are we talking about your mom right now?"

"Before I left, she took me aside and told me I could stay over if I wanted – it wouldn't bother her."

"Really?"

"You sound shocked."

"I am, a bit. It would feel … weird. Kind of disrespectful to your mom. And pretty obvious." I pause. "Except, of course, if you want to …"

He laughs. "No. I know what you mean. Although I do want to wake up with you one of these days."

"Did I mention I'm getting a single room in residence?"

"Now *that* is an interesting piece of information."

Chapter Twenty-Seven

W e're at the barbecue held at Lacey's every summer. It was at this party that I first met Lacey last year.

Jared hands me a cold can of Diet Coke. "So are you ready for the ride?"

It's twenty-eight degrees, and sunny, but I shiver. "I don't know."

"I didn't mean it that way. I know you're *ready*. I just meant, is everything actually set for the ride? Does Will have the music? Do you have a second trailer lined up? Is there anything you need your boyfriend to step up and do this week?"

"Boyfriend ... really?"

Jared frowns. "What else would I be?"

"The guy I can't resist? Whose kisses make me melt? Who I wish would bring me breakfast in bed next Saturday instead of us both rising with the sun to get to this musical ride? You're all of those things. It's just that we haven't used the 'boyfriend / girlfriend' terms, since, you know, *the break*."

"*The break*. Now there's a term I don't like." He leans in and kisses my nose and, right on cue, a wave of warmth washes through me. I'm turning my face up to get my mouth onto his, when a chorus of giggles stops me.

Carly, Lacey, Alanna, Bridget. All together. All grinning. Thank goodness. I've got to hand it to Bridget – she's really earned her way back into their trust.

"Aaaahhh …" I turn to Jared. "That reminds me. There is one thing I haven't done."

"Does that mean it's time for The Package?"

"Definitely."

"OK, I'll meet you at the barn."

"What do you mean, Meg? What package?" Lacey's holding my arm. "What's up?"

"Go find Will, and bring him to the barn, and you'll find out."

The four girls are crowded onto a bale of hay sitting in the barn entrance. "Aw, look at you guys …" I pull out my phone and snap a picture.

"Come on Will; stand behind them." He overbalances, and puts his hands out to steady himself. One hand lands on Lacey's shoulder; the other on Bridget's. I click a shot.

I study both pictures. "Those are nice, but there's something missing." They all look around, at themselves, at each other, then turn blank faces to me.

"The horses?" Carly asks.

I turn to Jared, who's holding a cardboard box. "Hey, *boyfriend*, do you know what's missing?"

He grins. "I think I might."

I open the flaps on the box, and pull out a neat, dark, jacket with **WEDNESDAY WONDERS** embroidered on the back, arched over an outline map of the island.

I hold it up, display the front and back, and more than one of the girls gasp.

"Oh!" Lacey says. "Oh! Oh! Oh! Are those for us? They're *awesome.*"

Jared and I hand them out. One for each rider, and one that says **TEAM SUPPORT** on the back for Will.

I take a step back, and reach for Jared's hand, and look at the group; all neat, and matching. Turning each other around to look at the back of their jackets. Talking. Getting along. And I realize they're not a group anymore. They're not "the girls" or "my riders" – they're a team.

They've grown into a team, and I'm so proud of them.

Chapter Twenty-Eight

I'm less of a coach, more of a logistics coordinator, getting four girls and four horses to a fair on the mainland on the same weekend I'm also moving into residence.

We leave in convoy. Rod's hauling one two-horse trailer. Jared and I are pulling another. My mom and dad's car is jammed with the things I'm supposed to need to get me through my first year at school.

As the ferry nudges into the dock on the Kingston side, I say good-bye to my parents. "Thank you so much for doing this. Just dump the stuff in my room as it is. Don't try to organize it. You know how to get to the fairgrounds?"

The girls' eyes go wide and then glaze over as we unload the horses with a Ferris wheel off to our left, and the sounds and smells of the fair starting up all around us.

"Lacey and Carly, help us fill the haynets. Bridget and Alanna, get water. Then go for an hour. Explore. Get it out of your systems. Jared and I will watch the horses."

Will sticks his head out of the back of the trailer he's been sweeping clean. "Can I go too?" he asks.

Rod nods. "Yup. Better catch them."

We watch him run off, then collapse into the camp chairs Rod's brought. Jared's mom has sent coffee in a Thermos. Betsy's sent muffins.

The horses swish their tails at flies and munch on their hay. Jared reaches for a third muffin. Rod pours a fourth cup of coffee.

Rod lifts his Thermos cup. "Quite a summer."

Jared swallows a bite of muffin. "Quite a summer."

I sip from Jared's coffee, and the bitterness waters my eyes. "Quite a summer."

Rod looks up. "Here they come."

Show time.

Except not all of them have come back. Alanna, and Carly, and Lacey tumble into the area between the two trailers giggling and showing off bracelets they bought with their horses' names engraved on them. Alanna hands one to me that reads **JESSIE**.

"Oh, it's really nice." I hand it back to her, and she shakes her head.

"No, I got two. That one's yours."

Suddenly my eyes are full of tears. I swallow hard. "Wow … I love it." I snap it on my wrist and give Alanna a hug. Her shoulders are so thin, but she's been strong this summer. They all have. Which makes me think of the most strong-willed one of all. "Does anyone know where Bridget is?"

Three shaking heads.

Great. Just what I need is Bridget acting up here, now.

"You three go ahead and start getting ready. I'll go look for her. If you have any questions, ask Jared, OK?" I find his eyes, and he nods.

OK. Here I go on a Bridget hunt.

I walk along the back of the parked trailers, looking down rows, but why would she be at another trailer?

Glance out to the main ring, where the classes haven't started yet, so it would be easy to pick her out of the few, straggling people standing around. She's not there.

The rides aren't open yet.

I know, for sure, the girls were by the barn filled with stalls selling jewellery, and cowboy boots, and candles, and anything and everything horse, or cow, or farm-themed. I walk through but, even though it's not as busy as it will be later in the afternoon, I don't see her.

She could be anywhere. And if she's doing something she's not supposed to be, she's not going to make herself easy to find.

I head out of the marketplace barn and glance down the narrow alley between it and the next barn over.

Bingo.

My heart double-thumps. Not just Bridget, but Will, too.

They're in the shadows cast by the overhanging eaves of the barn. Will's got his hands on her hips, and she's touching his cheek.

I step back, out of their line of sight.

I *so* don't want to interrupt them.

But time's ticking.

Two guys walk by. Young. Wearing jeans and cowboy hats.

"Excuse me?"

They have freckled faces, big smiles. They seem right for the job.

"Would you mind cutting between these two barns? Any maybe just making some noise on your way in? It would be a big help to me."

One guy raises an eyebrow, takes a couple of steps sideways to look down the passage, then comes back with an even bigger grin. "Sure, I think we can probably do that."

"Thanks! You guys are life-savers." I turn to head back to the trailer.

Behind me, I hear some hooting, then, "Whoops! Excuse us!"

I quicken my pace. That should get Bridget and Will moving, and I want to make sure I'm back when they show up.

***

There's nothing I can do now but hold my breath, cross my fingers, and smile so the girls will always see a happy face if they look my way.

I stand by the in-gate and say, "Good luck," and then step to the side and watch as they ride in two-by-two, neat, professional, and cohesive in their matching jackets.

The girls line their horses up on the centre line, Will hits the music, and they go.

The horses' steps sync up perfectly with the beat of the music. I know Alanna's doing everything she can to slow Jessie, and Carly's chasing Shelby, but nobody else can tell.

Their circles are perfect, and they spiral in and back out at the same time. It looks better than I even thought it would.

The intertwined serpentine is by no means their hardest move, but it looks tricky.

It's a simple routine, but each horse does every move properly. Bending, flexing, listening. The girls are careful, and accurate. It makes all the difference.

There's a bobble in the cross-over. Jessie's going way too fast, and she's not going to leave the gap Bridget needs to take Diamond through. I watch as the normally quiet, relaxed Alanna gives Jessie a sharp half-halt, and the shocked mare listens, and drops back, and they finish the manoeuvre collision-free.

When they line up at the end, the audience is already applauding, and then Bridget rides Diamond forward and he bows down for her to step off.

Lacey takes her place, Diamond rises again, and Lacey stands.

She slips – the tiniest of bobbles that sends my heart into my throat. But rock-solid Diamond never moves, and Lacey straightens, then throws her arms out and grins.

I think the crowd claps even louder because of the near fall. Everybody loves a little thrill and the girls have delivered.

I'm so happy for the girls, who come in third. First place goes to a team sponsored by a car dealership who have not just matching jackets, and saddle pads, but matching horses; all bays, wrapped with colour-coordinated polos.

Somebody tells me the second-place team have practiced together for two years.

The island contingent is strong. Betsy and Carl, the girls' families, Jared's mom, my parents, and a few of the people who said they might come, are sitting in the stands. When the results are announced, they definitely make more noise than the other teams' fans.

We leave the girls at the cotton-candy, midway-ride, country-music, sensory overload that is the fair – with Will, of course – and Jared, and Rod, and I make sure all the horses get put back where they should.

I arrange saddles and bridles in Lacey's tack room then, instead of going straight to the truck where Jared's waiting, turn to the paddock. "Jess! Jessie! And you, too, Salem!"

Two heads pop up. Four ears are outlined against the sky. Jess whickers, and my heart squeezes. I love the way that sound, coming from deep inside my horse, also hits a spot deep inside me.

I meet the mares at the gate and duck through the fence to them. I slip them each a chunk of carrot and they take it and crunch it down before whiffling me all over for more.

I stand for a few minutes with Jess's face pressed into my chest and Salem huffing down my back.

"Good girls. Good, good girls."

Then I pull out the last two pieces of carrot I had stashed in my back pocket and hand them over, before running back along the driveway to Jared.

***

I'm tired by the time Jared and I drive back onto the ferry, heading for Kingston, for the second time today. The pizza we picked up in the village gives me a bit more energy and then, as we park several streets away and walk to my new residence – my new home – a surge of adrenaline chases away my last traces of fatigue.

The cars still lining the drop-off lane, and the people milling in the lobby, and the elevators jammed with mini-fridges, and hockey bags, and laundry hampers, make the residence seem even bigger than when I first saw it. Jared's eyes widen. "This place is *huge*."

I take his hand. "You'll get used to it. I guess I will, too."

Closing my door behind us helps. The cinder block walls deaden any sound from either side, and the occasional laughing drifting through the window, and the muffled bumps and voices that penetrate through the door, are distant enough to give us some peace.

I feel like I can join the activity anytime I want to, but I don't have to.

And I definitely don't want to right now.

"So," Jared raises his eyebrows. "A single bed."

"Think you can handle it?"

He wraps me in his arms, then trips me so I fall onto the mattress. "I think it'll help me get as close to you as I want to."

He kisses me, and I kiss him back. Then we kiss so that everything melds together and it's impossible to say who starts or finishes any one of the long kisses that run into each other.

Jared stops, and rolls his weight back, then reaches into his pocket.

"Hey! Come back here …" When his hand appears holding a small box, the breath whistles out of me. My pulse goes from quick to overdrive. I was hot just a second ago, but now I'm freezing cold.

"Meg? Meg! Don't freak out. Smile. Breathe."

I inhale, then exhale. OK, I'm officially still breathing.

"What …?"

He grins. "I don't know whether to be flattered or upset at your reaction."

"I don't know what I'm reacting to." My voice doesn't sound like my own. It's the voice of a girl who's trying to be cool, and funny while wondering if her life's about to change.

"Well, I noticed you stopped wearing your leaf necklace."

My hand flies to the bare skin above my t-shirt collar. "It was just because the chain broke. It wasn't ..."

"I know."

"How did you ...?"

"I saw it on your windowsill when I was there the other day." His grin is sheepish. "And I kind of took it."

"You took it?"

He flicks the box open with one hand, and inside is my leaf pendant.

"Oh ..."

"Go ahead. Take it out."

I struggle to prop myself against the wall, and lift the shining leaf out. With it comes a sleek, new silver chain that glimmers in the daylight from my window.

"It's beautiful. It's new."

"The chain is new, and the pendant's been polished. So it's what you had, but better. Do you like it?"

I grip the chain in my fist, wrap my arms around his neck, and pull him close.

What I had, but better.

"It's absolutely perfect. I wouldn't want anything else."

About the Author

Tudor Robins is the author of books that move – she wants to move your heart, mind, and pulse with her writing. Tudor lives in Ottawa, Ontario, and when she's not writing she loves horseback riding, downhill skiing, and running.

She's also written:

Objects in Mirror
Appaloosa Summer (the first book in the Island Trilogy)
Hide & Seek (a stand-alone short story)

If you'd like to be automatically notified of Tudor's new releases, please sign up at: http://tudorrobins.ca/newsletter-signup/.

Word-of-mouth recommendations from readers like you allow Tudor to sell her books and keep writing. If you enjoyed this book, please consider leaving a review on Amazon or Goodreads. Even just a few words really help. Your support is greatly appreciated!

Say Hi!

I love hearing from my readers. You can connect with me through my website – www.tudorrobins.ca – find me on Facebook or Twitter, or email me directly: tudor@tudorrobins.ca.

Acknowledgements

Once again, this book would not exist without the inspiration, peace, and writing time I get when staying on Wolfe Island.

This book would also not be anything like the story you've just read without the time, care, consideration, and input of my incredibly committed, and talented editor, Hilary Smith.

Allie Gerlach delivered another great Island Trilogy cover, Gillian Campbell rooted out my mistakes and typos, Cheryl Perez provided the great layout for the print book, and Lynn Jatania of Sweet Smart Design made sure the website matched the energy of the new book.

Made in the USA
San Bernardino, CA
12 May 2017